STOLEN BY THE ZANDIAN

RENEE ROSE

REBEL WEST

BURNING DESIRES

CHAPTER 1

*K*ailani
        *If I don't escape my jailers before tomor-
row's auction, I'm dead.*

"We'll get a fortune for her. I can feel the stein." The Caretaker's gruff laugh makes my muscles tense. He waves his six-fingered hands as if ushering in the glittering coins.

My stomach churns.

"We can charge anything. The Ocretions are desperate to reverse engineer her for her antiviral properties to eliminate disease in their human slaves." The Overseer giggles, a sound that doesn't match his thick, warty body. "We can retire."

"We have the most valuable commodity in the galaxy."

The two Kraa eye each other across the battered table; despite their boastful banter and their matching green skin, it's obvious they have zero trust. Their alliance is forged on greed and desperation–and I'm the unfortunate item they plan to sell at auction.

I pull back from the peephole high in the wall of my holding cell and spider-walk down the cement walls by digging my bare fingers and toes against cracks in the rough

1

texture. My bio-enhanced muscles and tendons allow me to climb surfaces that are unscalable by normal humans.

When I'm three feet from the ground, I twist and leap silently to the packed earth floor, landing without effort, fingertips of my left hand just skimming the dirt. My curls swing and sway around my shoulders.

My cell is pitch black, but my eyes were enhanced through a particularly painful procedure several sun cycles ago, so my new rods and cones can pick out the faintest traces of light. "Just like a wild animal," the Medical Manager described me with pride as I was displayed to a secret group of Kraa politicians.

I pace the room on soundless feet. The Ocretions are known to be brutal to their human slaves and are eager for ways to make them work harder, longer, faster. What the Overseer meant by the euphemism of reverse engineering: The Ocretions will perform experiments on me to assess my enhanced human functionality then dissect me.

If I enter their custody, the rest of my short life won't be good. Not that it's amazing right now–

I breathe deeply to force back panic, in and out, until my heartbeat is slow and even.

"You can do this," I recite the mantra inside my head. "There is nothing unreachable to those who have courage."

Another female human slave, an early prototype of me, whispered it to me one day during a lesson. That was prior to her death on the Kraa operating table.

She said it was an ancient human phrase uttered by a wild and victorious king, and that from the earliest of origins, we had powerful ancestors who never gave up. She urged me to tell any and every human I ever found.

I hear the rumble of continued conversation, so I clamber

back up the wall to peek through the small gap between the metal beams.

My owners stand together at the door, the yellow light making their skin sallow and accentuating the pocked eruptions on their faces. They may be the last few Kraa alive in this galaxy, but right now, it doesn't matter if there are two of them or two million: While I'm locked up in their custody, I have no future.

"Do you have the stash of her medicine?" The Overseer's eyes dart around the room. "Without it, the buyers won't pay top prices."

"Of course I have it." The Caretaker is testy. "But you don't need to know where." He chuckles. "Don't bother looking for it. You won't find it." He puffs up his chest, a typical Kraa display of power.

"Withhold the drug for sundown." The Overseer's face goes from frustrated to neutral. "Without it, she'll be incapacitated. We'll give it to her while she's in cuffs at the auction, so buyers can see that she's functional."

"I concur." The Caretaker laughs. "Let her suffer tonight. It will make her more pliable." They leave the room, and the door clicks shut behind them.

I suspected they were going to do this, and yet the burst of anxiety that floods my body is nearly unbearable. I barely make it to the floor this time and curl up on the hard cot.

This cell may be imperfect, but it's hardy enough to keep me captive, even with my enhanced strength. There's no way I can tunnel or break through the thick walls, especially not once the crippling migraine headache begins.

Already it's starting to pulse behind my eyes, trickles of sensation flowing like ice water through my skull. Soon I'll be writhing in pain, blind from the agony. They designed me this way, to be dependent on the medicine, and without it, I can't survive.

"There is nothing unreachable," I mouth. I have about fifteen minutes before it hits, and I'll use every single second to reformulate my escape plan.

They designed me, but they don't control my mind. And I'd rather die during a failed escape attempt than go into Ocretion ownership.

I count the time even as I think, my neurons working overtime. I wind my fingers together and stare into the black. "There is nothing…"

And then the wave of pain washes over me, and I'm gone.

KHRYS

"I heard what happened." Arnie, the Zandian warrior beside me shakes his head. "I wouldn't want to be in your boots when you talk to King Zander." He wipes his arm along his smooth purple forehead. One of his horns was smashed during the war to recapture our planet, and it leans to the left. "Especially with what's going on with the King's young— and all the half-breeds on the planet taken ill. He's not going to have any patience for mistakes."

I swallow. It's true—a sickness has overtaken most of the young on Zandia—all the half-breeds are ill with it, and despite the work of Dr. Daneth and all the medics, a cure hasn't yet been found. Every being on the planet is on edge about it. The thought of our already near-extinct population losing its newest generation is devastating.

Veck.

I glower at him. "It was an accident." My voice is curt. I already can't stand myself for the destruction to the Zandian ship while trainees were under my watch. I sure as *veck* don't want to answer to this jaghole about it. Not when I'm about to face the king, himself.

The truth is, It was an accident that could have been prevented had I not frozen.

"It's not the first accident under your watch." He eyes me. "Maybe it's time for you to find a new position."

"*Veck* off."

"No offense." He shakes his head. "But it would be for the good of every being. Think of the damage done to the confidence of the trainees who wrecked. Your job is to provide them successes, not failures."

My fingers curl into fists, and I leave Arnie without answering.

"It wasn't your fault," he calls to my back. "What happened to your brother. But this is. You need to get your head on straight, warrior."

I want to kill him for mentioning Kyl, my younger brother, who died during the battle to reclaim Zandia.

It *was* my fault. I was the one who commanded Kyl, and if I'd done a better job, he'd still be alive now.

Grinding my teeth, I head towards the royal dwelling, dusting off my tunic and straightening my sword as I enter the palace. I nod to the guards at the door. Better to get this over with.

I wait outside the throne room until I'm summoned.

"My lord." I drop my eyes and lift my arm at a ninety degree angle in the traditional Zandian greeting, showing my deference and admiration for our fearless Zandian ruler. When I lift them, I see the king's face appears older. He's aged in the past six lunar cycles since the epidemic first hit our human population. His own daughter, Princess Kaylar, is said to be fighting for her life from the Z4-A virus. The adult humans have mostly been able to handle the virus, but it's our halfling population that's been hit hard.

"Captain Khrys." King Zander's voice is sharp and serious. "What happened?"

I look up and clear my throat.

Veck.

My species are known for being stoic and strong. Guided by logic not emotion. At least until they come in contact with a human female—or so the tales go.

But since Kyl's death, I'm constantly plagued with doubt. My decisions have become less logical and more impulsive, sometimes with devastating results.

"It was an issue with the navigation settings. I let my newest trainee handle the landing on his own. He entered the numbers on the test run this morning. I should have double-checked them, but I wished to show my confidence in his abilities. Unfortunately, his coordinates were off, and we brushed the landing gear on the craft."

"By brushed, you mean crushed?" The king raises his brow at me, his voice stern.

"Yes, my lord." I wince, thinking of the awful screech of metal, the smoking damage, and worse–the fact that the crew were, for no matter how short a time, in jeopardy. "Repairs are underway, and we'll be ready for testing tomorrow."

The king purses his lips. "This is the second incident of this nature under your command."

"Yes, my lord." I bow my head. *Veck.* "It won't happen again."

There's silence for several seconds.

"No, it won't recur." The king raises his hand and gestures. "I'm replacing you as the Spacecraft Training Commander."

His words hit me like a blow to my gut. "But my lord–" I

break off. A Zandian does not contradict or argue with his king.

"The team has lost confidence in you." Zander's voice is even, but it sends chills into my horns." Can you think of a good reason I should not remove you?"

In my mind, I replay the cries of the crew and then their quick response. Luckily, the accident–as they go–was minor compared to what could have happened. But I didn't miss the expressions on their faces afterward.

I blink and meet his gaze. My voice is dull. "No. I cannot."

"Captain Rhob will take over, effective immediately. You will spend the necessary time to brief him. Then we will find you a position that better suits your talents."

"Understood." I keep my expression impassive, but flames of shame and regret lick my skin.

The king regards me. "We have no time for your deviations from protocol, Khrys."

"Yes, my lord. I will do better."

"See that you do." He looks at me for a second. "You are dismissed." He turns to his assistant, perhaps because he is truly busy but possibly to teach me a lesson about my place in his regard–which is clearly as low as a Zandian can fall.

I stride from the building, cursing my impulsivity. "*Veck, veck, veck*!" I stop and punch a tree, shredding the purple skin on my knuckles and causing lines of blood to well up. "*Veck* it all."

Honor is everything to a Zandian warrior, and I just lost what was remaining of mine.

I wipe the blood on my tunic and stare at the setting sun. My hand throbs, and I welcome the pain. I should cut my *vecking* arm off to teach myself a lesson about being a stupid idiot.

7

"You all right?" My friend Gabin stands a few feet away, perhaps cautious about approaching me in such a wild and unpredictable state.

I don't look at him. "You heard."

"I did." He shifts; I hear gravel crunch under his boots. "The crew will forgive you. They already have."

"King Zander reassigned me."

"Oh." He steps closer. "I see." He pauses. "Is there a way this can be a positive change for you?"

"Yes. It's a great thing when an expert training captain is removed from duty. We should have a festival. Celebrate my fall from grace." I glower at him. Once, sarcasm would have been foreign to me, but now that we have humans on Zandia, I've picked up the technique.

His voice holds reproach. "I thought perhaps the job was not a perfect fit."

"A Zandian does the job he is given and loves it because he is serving Zandia." My tone is stiff. "My father wanted me to be a training captain all his life, like he was. He sacrificed everything to get me into it and then died saving my life in the raids. Zandia has spent much time and effort on my training."

"I know." He comes closer.

"I've betrayed my father's memory. Let down my fellow Zandians."

Gabin stands beside me for a second, and neither of us speak.

I sigh. "I must go clean up." I look at my hand. "Then I'll speak to–" my wrist holo blinks green with an incoming message from– "Captain Rhob. He's eager to get started."

Gabin claps my shoulder. "Khrys, you're a good Zandian. You'll find your place."

He means well. But the words twist a dull knife deep into

my gut because they only cement into my mind what I and every being know: I don't fit.

"Regards," I snap and stalk off. I don't have the energy to show appreciation for his support.

Back at my domicile, I rinse my fingers and apply the healing salve created by one of the humans who works with Dr. Daneth, and in seconds, my wounds have sealed over.

The holo blinks again–*veck* that Captain Rhob. Of course, I correct myself, if I had such eager intensity for the job myself, I would probably not be in this excruciating situation of needing to train my own replacement. It's my own fault I didn't apply the right focus to overseeing my trainees. I don't know why I can't seem to stay razor sharp when I'm with the students in the craft–I know the rules; *veck*, I wrote them!

I shake my head. Well, I guess I don't need to worry about that any longer since I've been demoted.

Before I connect with Rhob, I glance at my tablet monitor, checking the research which occupied my mind last night and filled my thoughts this morning before the unfortunate maneuver. It's an image of a slave who's up for auction soon; I found it by searching hidden channels on the holo-stream.

The human female looking back at me from the screen is gorgeous. Long black curls, eyes the color of the blue grotto waterfalls, and skin like a Chari fruit, an even golden brown, she's one of the most breathtaking creatures I've seen.

But it's not her looks that have me hooked.

"Human Female, age 28 solar cycles. Enhanced bio-abilities," the dossier reads. "Muscle strength 1.75X strongest human female. Night sight ability. Lung endurance X 12. Fast twitch muscle reaction 8X stronger than best human on record. Gen-mod blood antibodies resist all known human viruses. Other details to serious buyers only."

Gen-mod blood antibodies resist all known human viruses.

That was the part that caught my eye. What if this specially-engineered human held the solution to the Z4-A epidemic in her cells?

The price listed makes me whistle and shake my head–it's a fortune. One could buy a planet for the stein. It occurs to me that maybe the owners plan to do just that.

The human's gaze is strong and almost angry. She may be a captive, but there's something in her expression that speaks to a strength that outlasts captivity–unless I'm imagining what I want to see.

And what I see in her picture is freedom: My freedom as well as hers. Last night, it was a wild idea. This planet rotation, it's my only chance.

If I can get this human for Zandia and if her body does hold the answers to the epidemic plaguing our new generation, my honor would be restored. Instead of being the *veck*-up, I'll be the brave warrior who sought a solution to a dire problem.

We Zandians breed with human females since most of our own females are long dead. If I could bring in this human and give her to Dr. Daneth, he could figure out what was done to make her immune to human diseases.

I hoped to obtain her as a side job; it seemed a good way to satisfy the emptiness deep in my core. It's absolutely not that my main job isn't–wasn't–perfectly satisfactory. As I told Gabin, Zandians are grateful for any job they are given. It's just…I want to be a contribution to Zandia, and I've lost my touch with training.

My wrist holo flickers a third time, and I close the picture on my tablet.

"Rhob." My voice is gruff as I connect with my peer.

"Meet me at the dome in ten minutes. We'll start the information download."

I grab my other tablet, the work one that contains flight sim data and training module information.

As I leave my domicile and stride over to the flight area, I keep envisioning the human's striking blue eyes. The set of her chin. The strength in her shoulders. Those frail human fingers, the ones that are half the size of Zandian hands. And although I know I'd be taking her for the good of Zandia, not as a mate, part of my body can't help but react to her beauty.

She's for Zandia, I remind myself. *Not for me. Don't get too excited.*

I should petition the king for permission to go off and secure her for Zandia. But considering what happened during this planet rotation, I doubt he would trust me.

So... I could go without leave. Not inform any being of my plan. I can use a borrowed Zandian crystal to attempt to buy the female. Better to beg forgiveness than ask permission in this case.

Yes. I have to make this work. It's the best chance to regain my honor and prove that I'm worthy of serving my planet.

ailani

The room swims around me. The scent of sweat—both human and alien—fills my nostrils assaulting my already churning stomach. My nails cut into the heels of my bound hands as I stumble across the polished stone floor of the trade center.

I've heard of this place. It's a high-end epicenter for gambling, auctions—especially of things illegal to trade on other planets—and distribution. The Caretaker and Overseer haven't given me the medicine to take away the migraine yet. It's part of controlling me. They're not going to risk my escape while I'm in transport.

I can barely see—the light feels too harsh. It cuts into my brain like a laser beam. They bring me to a roped off area and put me up on a marble dais.

The caretaker strips off my clothing and pulls my bound wrists over my head, where he attaches them to a hook that's too high. It pulls me up to my tiptoes.

He squeezes one of my lifted breasts with a grunt of approval. "They'll like that," he mutters. The Kraa weren't interested in me sexually, so this assault is the first of its kind, but if I don't get out of here, it won't be the last. But then, I won't be sold as a sex slave. No, that would be a blessing after the life I've had. I'll be sold as a medical oddity for examination and dissection.

He spins me around to examine my backside. He slaps my ass a few times, not punitively, more like he's watching it jiggle.

"Please, Master. My medicine," I beg. I'm not even pretending. I really would grovel at his feet for even a portion of the medicine I need to take away the headache.

He takes out the little vial, uncorks it, and dribbles two drops—half the dosage—into my mouth.

I moan, my body trembling for it. I hang on my bound wrists and close my eyes, waiting for it to take effect.

"How much for the human?" I hear a deep voice ask.

"Oh, she'll fetch more than all the slaves in here put together," the overseer boasts. "She's been genetically modified. She's stronger and more durable than most humans. Capable of working five times as hard as the average human slave. Immune to illness, too."

"Wouldn't a slave-master wish his slave to be weak? Easier to control?" the male asks. There's a deceptively casual note to his accented words that make me crack my lids to take a peek.

He's not Ocretion or Kraa. I don't know what species he is—I've never seen one like him. He's larger than the Kraa with purple skin, stubby horns on the top of his head, and broad shoulders. He carries a sword at his belt. He's some kind of warrior.

"Not for your kind," the caretaker scoffs. "Besides, she requires a dose of medicine twice a day. That need keeps her exceedingly obedient."

I grind my teeth at his nasty smile.

The white-clad warrior scans me with seeming disinterest, yet for some reason, I have the feeling it's an act.

"May I approach her?" he asks. There's a regal quality to his voice, like he's used to being in command.

Oddly, I find it exciting. Or maybe it's just that the medicine's starting to work, and I can see him more clearly now. He's beautiful—square jaw, smooth, hairless skin, warm brown eyes.

I expect him to squeeze my breast, as the caretaker did, but instead he puts a knuckle under my chin and nudges it up, turning my face from side to side to inspect me. "She's in need of this medicine now?"

My heart picks up speed that he noticed. I haven't had masters who noticed or cared about such things before, except to torture me. And maybe that's all this male would want to do, as well, but for some reason, I find myself wondering what it would be like to have such a strong, virile male as my master.

Would he use my body for things other than hard labor?

Would he be gentle? Take care of my needs the way no one has before?

But that's ridiculous.

I'm not sticking around to be some horned alien's slave.

I'm going to escape. Get to Jesel where they say humans live free.

"She's been given a half-dose, so she presents well," The overseer says.

"Why not a full dose?" the purple warrior asks. He runs a thumb across my lower lip.

Surprised by the unexpectedly pleasurable touch, I part my lips and meet his gaze.

"We've found keeping her needy ensures her good behavior," the caretaker says silkily.

"She appears sickly," the male snaps. "How do I know you're not actually trying to get rid of an ailing human with limited abilities?"

"We have holo vids showing her in action." The caretaker flips open a small device. On it, I see myself lifting, leaping.

"Could be faked." The warrior narrows his eyes. "She can barely stand."

The overseer strides over, the wart on his cleft nose twitching. "Give her the rest of it." He jerks a hand at the caretaker, who shrugs and pulls out the vial.

Well. This is going better than expected. I would celebrate more if I didn't suspect the horned male had just manipulated them into this. Which leads me to wonder what his angle is.

I swivel toward the caretaker, walking on my tippy toes to try to get closer. My left nipple brushes against the purple-skinned male's white tunic. He doesn't move back. His eyes dip to my nipples, which tighten into stiff buds, as if preening under his gaze.

His hand lightly settles on my waist, and his horns thicken and lean in my direction.

If I weren't so desperate to get the rest of my dosage, I'd savor the fact that the attraction between us is mutual.

Not that I care about such things since I'm about to escape.

I open my mouth like a baby pet, straining at my bonds, so I don't miss a single drop. The caretaker dribbles it onto my tongue, and my throat works as I swallow.

"You were pretty desperate for that, weren't you, little human?" The horned stranger's thoughtful gaze rests on my face. He appears almost fascinated by me. For the first time in my life, I wonder, briefly, if I'm nice to look at.

All these years, I was bred and modified to be stronger and more resilient to damage. My looks weren't part of the Kraa enhancements. But the way the warrior looks at me, it's almost as if he finds me… attractive.

He raises his voice to speak to the overseer but doesn't turn away from me. "And how expensive is this medicine of hers? That's certainly a factor to consider, isn't it?" He's bargaining for me like I'm nothing more than the object I've always been to my masters, yet his steady regard takes away the sting of it.

Like he really sees me.

Me, not the enhancements. Not what I can do or what I'm useful for.

"She'll be sold with a lunar cycle's supply. After that, the medicine can be purchased from us, or for a higher price, the formulation and ingredients can be purchased for her new owner to make the elixir himself."

The warrior scoffs. "I asked the price."

"Fifty stein for a lunar cycle's supply."

Fifty stein.

Sweet Mother Earth, how will I survive? I won't be able to pay that. Nor will I be able to simply order it from the Kraa after I run away. They'd hunt me down. And the sentence for runaway slaves in this galaxy is death.

I'll just have to learn to live with the headaches. But even that thought brings back a stabbing pain behind my eyes and makes my stomach lurch.

"Where's this one month supply you say she'll be sold with?" the warrior asks.

Yes, where? I swear, it's like he's trying to help me escape. I watch the overseer's gaze dart toward the table and under it, I spy the padded case they carry the vials of my medicine in.

One lunar cycle's supply. It will have to do. Maybe I can just take micro-doses and get used to the migraines. So now I just have to crawl this wall to unhook my hands—that should be easy—then grab the medicine and run.

It's not great, as far as plans go, but I'll figure out the rest as I go. A distraction is what I really need. Something to give me a head start.

An amplified announcement comes from the stage. The auction's about to begin.

"Step away from her," the overseer snaps, spying the warrior's hand still resting on my waist. He slides it down to the top of my buttocks before he slowly pulls it away, his fingers trailing my skin like he doesn't want to stop touching me.

Goosebumps lift on my arms, and my skin tingles where his hand was. I register the loss of his nearness like a tiny panic. But that doesn't make sense.

The only panic I should have is over getting myself out of this place. He steps back out of the cordoned off area and folds his arms across his massive chest, subtly keeping me in his visual field while angling his body to the stage.

The caretaker lifts my roped wrists off the hook and clamps a hand around my upper arm, pinching my flesh as he roughly pulls me toward the stage. Sweet Mother Earth, this is probably my only chance.

I half-expect the purple, horned warrior to follow and bid on me. Not that I'm disappointed he doesn't. It's not like I'm going to walk out of here with a new master. Not if I can help it.

We stand behind the dais, waiting in the queue to go on stage. I look over involuntarily, searching for the purple warrior, but he's gone.

And that's when I act. I spin and whirl, using all the

fighting techniques they stupidly taught me, and in seconds I'm free. And that's when the artificial lights cut out.

KHRYS

AFTER CUTTING the power to the lights, I grab the medical case from under the Kraa's table. Zandians see better in the dark than most species, but I can't bank on the fact that I'm the only one who can see.

Still, I can't locate the female. She's not with her Kraa master. That part doesn't surprise me. She had the determined look of a warrior about to wage war. I was eighty percent sure she'd try to escape.

That's why I cut the lights—to provide a distraction, if not the means.

I also made sure she received her full dosage of medicine. Those Kraa bastards had abused the poor human—that much was obvious. If I had time, I'd make them suffer for their treatment of her, but I don't.

I need to find the superhuman and convince her she's coming with me.

Which shouldn't be too hard considering I have the medicine she requires.

There. I spy a dark form moving along the wall in a decidedly unhuman way.

Fascinating.

She's making her way right toward her Kraa masters—returning for the medicine, no doubt.

I find my way to her and grasp one of her ankles, giving it a sharp tug, so she falls into my arms. She smells sweet, like sugarfruit and the Zandian starshine. She struggles against my hold, striking me in the face with the heel of her hand.

"I have the medicine," I tell her.

She goes still.

I flip her across my shoulder, so she's easier to carry. "You're leaving with me."

CHAPTER 3

K̶ailani
        His words stun me into silence. I barely register the touch of his powerful hand on the bare skin of my legs, the way my body presses into his more powerful one. He moves deliberately through the darkness. Around us, shouts of confusion and command ring out.

"Who are you?" My whisper is hoarse. I twist my torso to look around. "Put me down."

He adjusts his grip on my body and slaps my naked ass once with his free hand—hard. "No, my marvelous little warrior. You're mine now."

I've been damaged and abused beyond imagination by my Kraa owners, but the spank from this purple warrior is different. It sends tingles into my belly and causes my nipples to harden. So does his deep velvety voice. I somehow latch onto the *marvelous little warrior* part rather than his assertion of ownership—the part I should be worried about.

I block those thoughts and focus. "I'll pay you to set me free. We can come to an arrangement." Working on instinct, I slide my hand down his back and cup his buttock. I've never

21

been used as a pleasure slave, but the movement is almost natural. My fingers linger. Stars, his body is nice to the touch.

His laugh is quick. "That we will. And I set the terms, little warrior." He regrips me again and gives me another firm spank that goes straight to my feminine parts. "Don't test me."

I blink once, and the remnants of my headache disappear. My mind races. Once we reach the exit of the auction, I will attack him using my quick punch power, steal my medicine and whatever goods he has. Or even better—I'll take his craft. I've never been trained to fly one, but I've had brain tweaks that make me learn ten times faster than most humans. He's so strong, but I need to defeat him—it's my only chance at freedom.

"*Veck*." His voice is low and urgent. His body stiffens up. "They're blocking the exit."

"Bigger problem." My eyes, quickly acclimated to the dark, have found a more urgent threat. "Behind us, fifty paces, closing fast. Two Ocretions with laser guns." I do the math. "They'll be on us in ten seconds. They have night vision headsets."

My body fills with adrenaline. "Put me down—I've trained for this."

His laugh is harsh. "You? A human slave, taught to fight?"

"Yes. But we don't have time to discuss it." I snap his words back at him. Early on, the Kraa put me through holo attack simulations to test out my reflexes. "We fight together, or we both die."

For a painfully long moment, he hesitates. Then I'm on my feet, head spinning as blood rushes down to my limbs.

"Go," he snaps. "Now."

I don't need encouragement. I crouch and leap, turning

the side of my foot, so the heel bone smashes the nose of the closer Ocretion. I immediately repeat the move; this time, his facial flesh is already pulpy, and my foot comes away slick with blood. His scream of pain and fear soothes my ragged nerves, and he drops in the dark, a useless sack of flesh. The second one is easier to fell; his surprise makes him stand still and stare while I crack his trachea.

"Mine are down. I'm ready," I whisper, my voice hoarse with adrenaline.

At my back, the purple warrior grunts. The clang of steel on metal tells me he's unsheathed his wicked dagger from his waist and is fighting with a guard; the horrified squeals are a welcome notification that his attackers have been vanquished.

He breathes hard as I dart to his side. "Come." He grabs my arm. "On my signal, we run."

I don't argue because equipment overhead groans and whines, and then the lights flicker. The power is back.

"Go!" He tugs me, and suddenly we're racing, hand in hand towards the door. He's fast—so swift, I can barely keep up, so I focus and summon my burst powers, my surplus energy stores that allow me to push my human body harder than any being should.

"*Veck*, you're unbelievable," he mutters—I think. I can barely hear through the roar of the crowd, and my heart pounding in my ears.

I fly, faster and faster—I've never moved like this. Stars! It feels good. Even in the middle of this panic, there's something so intense and soul-satisfying to race on fleet feet with someone whose speed matches mine. For a second, I feel like the two of us are alone in the universe, our bodies working at their maximum capacity.

The fatigue hits me about thirty seconds later.

"Aiii," I gasp, my muscles locking so hard and tight that I

23

skin my feet on the hard earth as I tumble down. The pain is so intense that I see it blazing in front of me, white hot. My lungs are molten.

"*Veck*!" He stops and doubles back and scoops me up. "We're almost there."

I'm back over his shoulder now, head bouncing as he speeds to the tarmac. Our pursuers have multiplied; I count at least twelve beings bursting through the doors of the auction house.

"They have weapons," I croak. "laser guns. Long range. Through the pain, I narrow my eyes and estimate the trajectory. "Move to your left on my count. Three, two—*NOW*."

He jumps aside, and the beam of pure light crackles and sizzles past us, singing the hair on my arm as it heats the air with the power of a thousand bolts of lightning.

"Again, to your left. Now." I grab his waist to stabilize myself.

This time, the ray hits a nearby craft, a transpo vehicle. The smell of burning metal hits my nose as acrid smoke puffs up. Cries of rage and fear ring out.

"We're here." He stops in front of a sleek modern craft, and within seconds, I'm on the starship floor in a graceless naked heap, and he's seated at a high-tech control console. "Stay there and don't *veck* this up. We can die any moment," he snaps.

I'm about to reply when the g-forces hit me, pushing me into the wall with such immense pressure that my lungs empty of air, and I'm positive my stomach is touching my backbone.

I can't breathe—I'm going to pass out—when the craft suddenly goes weightless, and my body relaxes back into itself. I gasp out a long whistling burst and suck in oxygen, greedy for it.

My whole body is a wreck, full of cuts and bruises, but I'm alive. Safe. Away from the Kraa and the auction.

I glance up at my savior. His smooth purple brow is wrinkled in concentration, and the powerful muscles in his arms move as he taps and touches controls. I'm mesmerized by his face, stern and handsome; it evokes feelings I don't understand.

I struggle to sit up. "Who are you?" I shake my head. "What do you want with me?"

He finishes one last maneuver, then pushes his chair back from the screens and observes me closely. His purple horns gleam in the light, and his eyes darken.

Then he smiles. "Who am I?" He raises a brow and crosses his arms. "I'm Khrys. I'm a Zandian warrior… and your new master, at least temporarily."

Khrys

The little warrior doesn't appear to like this answer. She pushes to a sitting position, wincing. "I belong to no one but myself." Her voice is haughty and at odds with her subservient position. She grabs a silver foil blanket from her side where I tossed it and pulls it over her torso and lap.

My mouth twitches with a smile—an unfamiliar sensation. "What, for all of…" I pretend to count on my fingers. "One, two, three whole minutes?"

She glares at me. "I could have escaped by myself."

"No." I shake my head. "Not without your medicine. Without my assistance, you'd likely be back in chains. Or dead."

"Well, without *my* help, you'd be nothing but a pile of purple goo on the auction floor."

My lips tug again. "Doubtful." I like her spunk.

She sticks up her chin. "And right about now, they'd be washing your organs out the door with a power hose for all the vermin to enjoy."

I stifle a full smile. "Perhaps you played a minor role in my escape."

"*Our* escape. And if by minor you mean major, then yes. I agree." She narrows her eyes and glances around the craft area.

"Don't even think about it," I warn.

"By *it*, do you mean save your life again?" She puts a hand down to brace off the floor and gets slowly to her feet. "Ow." She winces and drops the cover as she reaches for her largest cut. "Oh, ow."

I'm up in a flash and at her side. Mainly to prevent her from doing anything rash, but I'm also concerned about her health. Super-engineered she may be, but she's still mortal—and humans are far more fragile than Zandians. "Let me see."

"Don't touch me." She shoves my hand away from her leg.

I catch her gaze, raising a stern eyebrow. "Behave yourself, little warrior. I will do what's necessary to see to your health. You will not fight me."

My breath hitches when I notice her nipples stiffen at my admonishment. I shouldn't be surprised. Our species learned great compatibility with the human females due to their love of our sexual dominance. Her breath quickens.

My horns stiffen and lean in her direction. "I'm your master now. You will submit and obey." *Veck*, those words make my cock rock hard. This beautiful slave is my ward for the moment. "But don't be afraid. A good master takes care of his prize."

And this one is a prize indeed. Beautiful. Bold. Incredibly strong and fast. Highly intelligent.

I wish I could keep her for myself—mate her and see what sort of halflings we could produce together. But halflings are the reason we need her. She's not for breeding. She's my offering to Zandia to get back into King Zander's good graces. To prove myself worthy again after my recent failure.

I keep one hand firm on her left shoulder and run the right hand over her calf, stopping before I touch the wound. "I have a medical kit that can help."

"I'm not a prize...not a possession," she asserts, but she sounds breathless. Her pupils are dilated, and her gaze keeps sweeping over my chest, shoulders and arms. "I don't need your—*oh.* A med kit. That sounds acceptable." Her cheeks flush, and she looks away.

I retrieve it from the side of the station and apply the salve and bandages and give her a fluid tube. I show her how to attach the upper-arm patch that seeps nourishment and medication through her skin; it will time-release the right dosage, so she can heal and regain strength. "This will help until we get back to Zandia. Dr. Daneth can make sure—"

She flinches. "No doctors. Where are you taking me?" Her voice rises with fear. "No—I'm not going anywhere with you."

"Oh, you're not?" I smirk. "How do you plan to get away? And then where exactly are you headed?" I quirk a brow. "And how will you get there? Perhaps you have a secret craft in the pocket of your—oh, but you're naked, aren't you?" I tsk. "

Ah, yes—she's *vecking* naked. As if I weren't acutely aware of that delectable fact.

Now that we're safely hidden in the vast expanses of

27

hyperspace, away from our pursuers, and the craft on autopilot, her beauty hits me with full force.

Her dark curls fall in front of her slender shoulders. Her body is lean and muscular with perfect round breasts and pink-brown nipples that make me want to grab her and do unspeakable things right here on the floor of the craft. My cock and horns get hard, and I turn aside for a moment to gain control.

When I look at her again, she has the blanket back and has wrapped it around herself in an ad-hoc gown. Her golden skin is flushed. "I could have managed." She looks around the area again.

She's clearly assessing my craft even as I have the total upper hand. I'll have to watch this one—she probably has escape plans already forming in her beautiful head.

"You have no chance against me," I advise.

"Didn't my assessment skills save you not once but twice from a long-range weapon?" She raises her brows.

"You were incredible," I admit.

She blinks as if she's never received a compliment before. Her color returns to normal again, and her breathing evens. Her own strength and the med kit have clearly helped her recover. "Well, then. Let's call it even, and you set me loose on the next habitable free planet." She glares at me and taps her foot.

"No chance, little warrior."

I didn't think she'd show abject submission and adoration, crying meekly and agreeing to my every suggestion. But she's far feistier than I could have predicted.

A fact that for some reason makes my balls ache. I need to regain the upper hand. There's no way I can get us safely back to Zandia unless she's docile.

"Let's get something clear." I step forward. "I recognize

your part in my—*our*—escape. But humans are not free in this galaxy. You are currently under my protection—and command. There's nowhere for you to go without a master, and I am your master."

I stare at her. As before, she turns pink under my gaze, and her thighs squeeze together. *Veck*—is she aroused? Yes, I believe her change in scent indicates arousal. I don't have intimate knowledge of human females, but these are universally understood tells. If I'm not wrong, this little warrior wants me as badly as I want her.

My voice gets husky. Perhaps I should apply a little gentle punishment to cleave her to me as master. "You will do as I say." My voice thickens with desire. I step forward another inch.

Her breath quickens, and her chest heaves. "I won't."

"Think logically." I make my voice silky, persuasive. "You have no other options. Things will be more pleasant if we get along." For a split second, my brain rushes to imagine just how vecking *pleasant* it could be. Thoughts of my lips on her pert nipples, my tongue in between her thighs, her pretty pink lips on my cock—

"I'll find a place where I can live as a free human," she retorts. "I've heard of some such planets." There's a slight quiver in her voice. Then, to my utter delight, she attacks.

"Hiyah!" she shouts and launches herself at me, twisting midair, so her fist gains momentum.

When her knuckles connect firmly with my jaw, I see stars. *Veck*, she's got moves! I grab for her body, but she's already danced away on the balls of her feet and dropped down into a warrior stance.

"*Stop.*" I bark the command as my skin throbs where she hit me. I'm not angry—she's a marvel to watch, and a little pain means nothing to a warrior. I'm more fascinated by her abilities. Delighted that I actually found this spectacular little warrior for Zandia.

She yells a battle cry and jumps again, but this time I'm ready. Even with her extra-human strength and her clever knowledge of body mechanics, she's no match for a Zandian warrior at full alert. I easily block and parry her strikes. I let her continue for a few more moments because, well, it's highly arousing. The blanket is on the floor, so she's fully naked and throwing herself at me.

"All right, that's enough, Kailani." The next time she strikes, I yank her into my body. I wrap my arms around her and pull her body tightly against mine, pinning her arms at her waist. I use one leg to wrap around hers and lower my head to lock hers against my chest.

She's completely under my control now.

My hands press against her bare skin.

"Bad girl," I murmur against her silky hair. "You must never raise a hand to your master." I hold her tightly.

Oh *veck*, now it's time for punishment. I shouldn't be so excited, but I am.

"Apologize for attacking me," I advise. "Swear it won't happen again." My body responds to her presence, and my cock gets iron hard once again, despite my best intentions to remain neutral. The urge to *veck* her is so powerful that I can barely stand it.

"You're not my master," she grits as she stamps on my boot with her bare foot. She kicks backward at my shin.

I bite back my chuckle. I'm supposed to be firm as her master. "You're going to be sorry you did that." I squeeze her against my chest as she wriggles in vain. "When you disobey me, you will pay the consequences."

She freezes, her head swiveling to look in the direction of

the cabinet where I locked her medicine. *Veck*, her Kraa masters really did use it to control her.

"No, not that," I soothe. "I think you'll find my punishments quite a bit more palatable. For both of us."

Veck—I can't wait to teach her a lesson in obedience. Zandians know there is one easy way to tame an unruly human, and usually results in both master and female feeling satisfied, even if the female ends up a little sore. I'm about to give it a try.

"Come, little warrior. Take your punishment." My voice is low and seductive as I walk her backward toward my flight chair.

"I'm not *little warrior*," she says, but her voice warbles. The sexual innuendo in my voice has confused her. Already, I sense the tension in her melting, as if her body is incapable of resisting.

"My name is Kailani." She sounds breathless. "Let me go or else I'll..." her voice trails off when I sit and tug her down —not too hard, but firmly—across my lap and put one hand on the small of her back.

"What are you doing?" She pushes and shoves at my body. In her alarm, she seems to have forgotten to finish her threat.

I'm already accustomed to her crazy strength, so it's easy enough to hold her in place. "I'm going to show you how human females are punished on my planet."

I raise my hand and bring it down on her pretty little ass with a hard crack.

"Oh!" she cries out, twisting and kicking her legs.

I adjust her to tuck her legs under one of mine. "Don't try to get away." I spank her again, hard, in the same spot. A patch of pink blooms on her taut skin. "I'll just spank extra."

"Um…"

I'm sure she's shocked by the sexual nature of the punishment. That seems to be the reason it works so well. No real harm is caused to the females, and their bodies are aroused by the submissive nature of it.

Still, this one fights her nature. "Stop it," she hisses, clawing at my calves.

I answer with a flurry of spanks on her ass and upper thighs.

"Oh! Ow. You— You—"

"My name is Khrys." I spank her again, right in the middle of both cheeks, over her glistening sex. "Remember that for your apology. Whenever you're ready, of course." I bring my hand down over and over until the pink turns deeper. "Keep your hands down. Scratching me means I double the punishment."

In response, she digs her nails into my skin so hard that she draws blood.

I hold her still with one hand and grab for a pair of magna-cuffs with the other. As the being with the upper hand, I find it easy to snap them onto her delicate wrists. "No more of that."

She starts to speak, but it comes out as a yelp as I commence spanking once again. I'm not using my full force, of course, but a hard Zandian palm can do a lot to a pretty little warrior ass.

"We will get a few things straight." I spank for emphasis. "You will listen to me and do as I say—our lives depend on it. I am your master and starship commander. If you refuse to comply, you will be punished." I spank again, nice and hard.

She squeals and tries to kick, but I've got her legs locked.

"Your bottom must be getting sore." I stop and rub her heated skin. Squeeze her lovely buttocks. "When you're ready to say you're sorry, I'm listening."

She doesn't answer. I hear the sound of her rapid breathing. "Fine," she mutters after a moment. "I'm sorry."

"For?" I squeeze her soft ass again.

She rolls her hips and lets out a little moan. "F-for attacking you."

"And?" I squeeze and rub some more. When she doesn't answer, I deliver a few more swats. Her buttocks clench and release. "For expecting you to be a decent being. I'm sorry I thought you'd do the honorable thing and set me free."

I stifle a chuckle. She's adorable. Quite mouthy for a slave—but she wasn't owned by Ocretions. She wasn't bred to serve, she was engineered by Kraa to fight.

My cock presses insistently against her hip, and I'm dying to move onto the more pleasurable part of punishment. Still, she hasn't surrendered yet. "Do I need to use my belt?"

The thought is enough to make my body come alive with pleasure. Disciplining this human is even more arousing than I'd expected.

"No." Her voice is suddenly quiet. "I won't do it again."

"And?"

"What else do you want?" Her tone rises in frustration. "Should I somehow bring you the universe on a platinum platter?"

I smile. Oh, stars. What I wouldn't do to own this little warrior and battle with her like this on a regular basis—of course, that's a ridiculous thought. She's not meant to be my mate. I'm going to deliver her right to Dr. Daneth and King Zander...once I get her back. That thought makes me uneasy. I expected a grateful human, happy not to be put into service by Ocretions. All the humans on Zandia are thrilled to be there.

This one, though? She already had plans to be free.

Granted, I doubt she would have accomplished it without my help, but I'm not sure she sees it that way.

Well, setting her free isn't an option. I wasn't lying when I said she wouldn't survive without a master. Humans are not a free species in this galaxy. Without a benevolent master, she'd live a far worse life.

Besides, If I don't bring her back with me, I will certainly face serious consequences for going on this mission without leave, on top of my already precarious position with the king.

She moves her body and her taut breasts push into the side of my thighs. The nipples are hard, and I have the urge to ease her down and take one into my mouth.

"Say my name." I bark the order.

"I forgot it. It wasn't memorable." She sniffs.

I grip a handful of her ass, squeezing roughly, then deliver, a nice sharp slap on her right cheek. "Yes, you do."

"Khrys!" she squeaks. "Khrys."

And suddenly the thoughts in my head change from just sexual to ones of protection. In an instant, just hearing her say my name brings up the fiercest protection instinct I have. I'd do anything to protect this little being from harm.

I rub her ass, soothing away the sting I inflicted. "Good girl."

She squirms on my lap. I pull her up to a sitting position and check her lovely face. "I'm the only thing between you and that." I point to the starship window, where the blackness of space is immense. One of my arms curls around her back, my hand strokes the place where hip meets thigh. "Look, there aren't even any stars in sight here. You can't survive right now without me. I don't care how smart you are—you can't operate this starship by yourself. You have nowhere to go. Attacking me would be death for both of us. Understand?"

She nods then breaks our gaze. "I understand." She sags against me, and my body revels in the sensation of her soft skin against mine. "Just, for a second there, I thought maybe…" she shakes her head. "Never mind."

"You thought what?"

"I thought maybe I had a chance to get away. That maybe my life could be different from what it was." I can barely hear the words.

Guilt burrows into my chest. Humans lead such difficult lives in this galaxy. On my planet, it's far better than anywhere else, but she couldn't possibly know or believe that.

"It will be different." I touch her chin. "Kailani." Her name feels good on my lips. "I'm not going to do to you what your previous masters did." I look into her eyes, so she can see my sincerity. "That I swear to you. I won't withhold your medicine. No harm will come to you."

She stares at me for a long minute. "Why *did* you take me?" Her voice is skeptical. "At such great personal risk." She looks around the craft. "And with such priceless tech. Your planet must find me valuable in some way."

Veck. She's right, of course. And I don't want to lie. But I also want her to trust me and my species more before I ask for her willingness to help.

I pause to find the right words to convince her. "Our planet needs humans." I eye her carefully, gauging her response. "Our species is nearly extinct. Only a handful of females remain alive. But we've found human females to be the next closest match for mating."

She stiffens. "I am not a breeding slave."

"No, no, no. That came out wrong. Humans aren't slaves on Zandia. Zandians on our planet take humans as mates."

Her blue eyes grow round. She swallows. "You want me as your mate?"

I don't know why I hesitate. I should have answered *no* immediately. But I don't. Maybe it's the way she's looking at me—like the idea is not repulsive to her. Maybe it's because the idea has been appealing to me since the moment I first saw her image in the advertisement for the auction.

But I can't. She's for Zandia not for me.

"No." I drop my gaze. "Not mine. On Zandia, humans have some choices about their existence. Yes, they require a Zandian guardian or mate, but they are not slaves."

"Oh." She's silent. "You could be lying."

I nod. "I could. I'm not. I can show you holos of humans on Zandia."

"Those could be phony."

I shrug. "Listen, Kailani. You and I both know I could put you into a cage and resell you like that." I snap my fingers.

When she winces, I feel like an asshole. "But I'm not going to. I'm taking you to my planet where you will be welcomed and treated far better than you would be by any other species."

She studies me.

"Every human on Zandia requires a sponsor. Someone who takes responsibility for seeing that they fit into Zandian society. I'm your master for now, and I need you to understand two things. One, I have superior power over you. Second, I won't use it to hurt you."

"You just spanked me." Her voice is reproachful, and she shifts on my lap.

I stroke the top of her buttocks and the side of her thigh to soothe her. "You attacked me," I remind her. "There are consequences." I bring my other hand to lightly cup her bare breast, brushing my thumb across it.

She swallows. "That wasn't very generous."

"No?" My lips quirk.

She rolls her hips on my lap, her breath quickening. "Y-you could have just asked me nicely to not attack you again."

I laugh. "That isn't in the warrior handbook."

I like her sense of humor because it brings out my own. This, too, is a new development for me: As Zandians, we are stiff and duty-minded. But the presence of human females on our planet has allowed even the bachelors, like me, to develop previously untapped regions of our personality.

"Did it hurt that much? Let me see." I flip her back over, easily handling her weight. I do want to check on her soft bottom and see if she needs soothing lotion, but truth be told, I'm eager to run my fingers over her body, to show her the rewards of submission.

The cuffs hit the side of my calf. I reach down to remove them and toss the shining bonds aside. She's far more docile now, and I don't want to bind her any more than necessary.

I brush my fingertips over her ass. "Nice and pink. You'll feel it later but just a bit." I don't know that from actual experience—I've never spanked a female before—but I've heard it said. The males in my species marvel at the wonder and beauty of the human female buttocks.

I rest my palm on her taut ass. "Just so you remember, this is what I'll do next time you claw me with your sharp nails or try to knock me down."

"But not if I try to grab your own sword and slice your arms off?" Her voice is teasingly hopeful. And then *veck* if she doesn't stick her ass up towards me, further into my palm, as if asking for another spank.

I hesitate. I've punished her; the thing is over. Except it clearly isn't. My cock hasn't received the message. And I scent the unmistakable arousal from between her thighs.

37

My little warrior liked what I did. And I think she wants more. This is the way Zandians have learned to master human females on my planet. Not through the cruel methods used by the Ocretions on their slave species but with sexual dominance. Light punishment in their erogenous zones. We bond them to us, and that bond becomes unbreakable on both sides.

"Any kind of de-limbing situation," I deadpan, "is absolutely off limits." And then I give her one more spank.

"Hmm." She wiggles. "Even if it's just one finger?" She parts her thighs just slightly. "Surely one finger doesn't do you much good."

I spank her again, a nice sharp slap, low on her buttocks. "Perhaps you don't understand the power of just one finger, Kailani? Let me show you what just one finger can do."

I push her right leg gently. "Spread wider, please." I help her shift her legs, so they're parted, the right one dangling slightly off my lap. Her pussy is dewy with moisture and the most delicate, provocative aroma. "Stars, little warrior."

Right now, she doesn't seem to mind the nickname. She hums slightly to herself, a low note.

I should not be doing this. Discipline is one thing, sexual contact is another. She's not my mate, and I'm not her master. I shouldn't be claiming her this way. I shouldn't even be thinking about her like this.

But I'm not going to stop. I stroke her hair with my left hand and slide the right one up her inner thigh. "Never underestimate the power of one thick digit."

As I speak, I glide my fingertip very slowly up her skin. "Sometimes it's the singular thing that can cause a climactic reaction."

She gasps and murmurs something and tries to wiggle closer to my hand.

I spank her again, hard, and hold her in place. "Stay where I put you," I tell her firmly.

She stops moving, so I touch her thigh again.

Her pussy is wetter than before, and she moans. "Khrys?" She grabs my leg, but this time it's a full-fingered hold. She's not trying to get away. It's more like she's anchoring herself to me. I like it.

I wonder if she's ever had an orgasm in her strange, difficult life. I don't care if this is wrong: I want to give her pleasure right now.

"Has any being ever touched you...like this?" I run my fingers so softly over her pussy that there's barely contact. Made you feel good?"

"No." Her voice is breathy. "I don't... I've never. They gave me hormone shots to ensure I wouldn't want to…" She lapses off. "But they must have worn off by now."

"Just relax into me." I stroke the small of her back. "Let the sensation grow."

She releases her muscles and sinks into my lap. "What are you going to do?"

I brush her labia softly. "This." I rub her soft, wet skin over and over. "And this." I work my way up and down her body. "A little of this."

She's breathing harder now. "Khrys…"

"And maybe, if you're very good...this." I tap her clit with my index finger.

CHAPTER 4

ailani

WHEN HE SPANKED ME, I was enraged—and then the feeling changed to something else. My whole body is on fire, little sparks darting and dancing along my nerves, all of the sensation culminating between my thighs. My ass tingles in a way that is undeniably pleasurable, and it begins to drive a need in my body for something more.

I've never felt this way before, and I don't want it to end. "Please." I push my hips upward to seek his magical finger. "Do it again."

He laughs. "This?"

Then he brushes my skin and rubs in that one little spot, the locus of my energy.

I practically scream with pleasure. "Khrys!"

"Shh," he soothes me, stroking my thighs. "This is just the start."

My breath comes faster, and I squeeze my eyes shut to

41

focus on the feeling. My body seems to know how to do this; I've spread my legs and tilted myself, so he can have better access.

"You see how just one finger can be quite...appealing?" He strokes me again, over and over. "Here...and here, too?"

Now he drives his finger deep into my cleft, teasing and touching, and my belly ignites.

I wail out my pleasure, squeezing my muscles as contractions of pure joy flow through and over me. It doesn't end; the sensation grows and swells, and when it culminates in a powerful burst of light, I almost pass out.

When I float back into my body and open my eyes, I'm sitting on his lap, my head on his shoulder, my arms wrapped tightly around him, as far as I can reach. His strong purple arms encircle me, and his breath is warm on my hair.

I stir. "Khrys?" I clear my throat. My bottom is a little tingly from the spanking, but that's mostly faded. The predominant sensation now is one of lingering pleasure and deep relaxation, the kind I've never known. It's fantastic. In fact, I already want to do it again.

Underneath me, his cock is rock hard. I reach down with one hand. "You didn't get to—"

I want to have that feeling again. I want more. I want to learn all about this new part of life.

But he's distant.

He gently separates himself from me and puts me down onto the bench beside him. "I should not have done that."

"I don't understand." I blink at him.

He stands up and hands me the silver blanket. "I have extra garments in a storage bin. I'll find some that fit you."

"But don't you want to..." —I tilt my shoulders— "...enjoy the pleasure as well?"

"It would not be appropriate." His voice is stiff. Almost

as stiff as the rod in his trousers. "I'm your temporary master —just until we reach Zandia."

"And what happens then?"

He turns away and rummages in a cabinet then places a stack of folded clothing next to me with a fluid tube and some nutrition packs. "Please get yourself together, and then we'll talk."

The craft interior isn't large, yet I feel alone over here on the bench while he sits at his flight console, staring out at the blackness around us. There are now stars visible, probably millions of light years away. Funny how he feels even more distant.

Well, it's better than a migraine... Taking a deep breath, I put on the sleek trousers and jacket. The boots fit me like a dream. And definitely an improvement over the Kraa cell.

Still, I don't know if I believe him about Zandia. I'm not sure he's telling me the truth.

But the buzzing pleasure still coursing through my body takes the sting away from captivity under his rule. It's a thousand times better than being owned by the Kraa or likely by any other master who would've bought me at auction.

I eye his broad back and shoulders. The thick horns on his head that seem to move and change depending on his feelings. I make a note to learn to read what those changes mean. What would it be like to be mated to a male like him? A male whose punishments are far more pleasurable than anything I ever endured before.

A shiver runs through my body, and my sex clenches at the idea of him claiming me fully. But he said he's just my *temporary* master. I don't know what that means, but I don't like it. Something far less pleasurable may await me on Zandia, and I need to be prepared for whatever that is.

I open a food packet and eat it while I sip on a fluid tube.

A few seconds later, the barest licks of sensation trickle along my temple. Fear lurches in my gut.

"Khrys?" I stand, fingers shaky on the fluid tube. My voice is high.

"What is it?" He whirls, expression concerned.

I touch my forehead. "It's starting again. I need the medicine." I hope to stars he will give me the dose I need.

"*Veck.*" He shakes his head. "Forgive me, I forgot."

The relief I feel at his instant response brings on a streak of gratitude. Maybe I can trust this warrior.

He turns to the console and taps then stands up and strides to a cabinet across from his flight seat. "I have your medicine supply here." He pulls out the sleek container. "I'll bring it to you. Sit down."

The whisper of pain deepens, little pinpricks. I press my palm to the top of my head, a useless move. Adrenaline races through my body. "Please hurry." My vision starts to blur. The stars outside the glass viewports, little dots of distant light, morph into blobs.

"Here." He's at my side. His hands are strong but so gentle as he touches my face. "How much?"

"Four drops." I close my eyes.

The bitter taste has never been so welcome. As the liquid hits my tongue, the relief is almost instantaneous: First, the aroma of herb and earth shoots into my nostrils, and then the pulsing pain flickers and flashes out. Gone.

I close my eyes and take a deep breath, licking my lips, even though he didn't spill. I swallow my own spit once, twice, to ensure that I've washed down every last remnant of the drug. When I look back, he's staring at me, brow wrinkled. Behind his head, outside in the emptiness of space, the stars are back to usual.

"Better?" He screws the dropper cap back onto the bottle. His eyes remain trained on my face, checking me.

I nod. "Yes."

He stows the glass bottle carefully into the case. "How does the medicine work?" He sits down beside me.

I watch as the small amber bottle nestles into the padding and shake my head. "They did something to my blood vessels in my head, the vessels feeding the brain. They constrict without the medicine, and it's painful. The antidote is made from the pollen of a flower found on Dentron. The medicine widens the vessels, but it's temporary."

"And without the medicine, the headaches keep coming back?" He touches my forehead softly, then pulls his hand back. Frowns. "Will they ever go away?"

Fear wells up. "Maybe over time, my body would adjust back, who knows? But I can't bear the pain to find out."

I think about suffering that kind of excruciating pain for many solar cycles. "I'd rather throw myself into the vacuum of space." My voice is fierce.

He starts like this surprises him. "Kailani, we have enough medicine for a while." He pulls the bottle back out of the case and holds it up at an angle to see how much liquid remains. "There's…" He pauses, clearly doing mental manipulations. "*Veck.* Only about ten more doses." His face grows somber. "How did they make it?" He takes my hand.

"We'd need the pollen to start." My body feels warm and tingly because he said *we. We have enough medicine.* I swallow hard and press his fingers against my own. "They mix it with a few other things, but the pollen is the main antidote. Once they ran low and gave me crushed heated pollen to eat, and it worked the same way although it took a lot longer and didn't get rid of the headache entirely. But still, it was remarkably effective even alone."

"And Dentron? Do you know much about it?" He does something on his wrist holo and pulls up a solar map. "It's near us." He sounds surprisingly pleased. "Within a half a planet rotation's flight."

"There's a tribe there who aren't technical, but they're hostile. We'd need to avoid them. Apart from that, I don't know much."

"They couldn't grow the plants on your planet?"

"No. I believe the environment wasn't right. I don't know much about ag, and they obviously didn't share much with me. But from what I gleaned overhearing their conversations, that was the problem." I try to remember every fact I committed to memory about the medicine. "But it probably wasn't a big priority, either. Without that medicine...Khrys? I'm as good as dead."

"Don't talk that way." His voice is low and fierce. "Look at me. Kailani? I'm going to get it for you."

"But when?" I shrug my shoulders. "After you take me to your amazing planet as a slave? I don't have that long."

"I told you, humans have good lives there. They aren't slaves." His voice rises with frustration, and he pulls his hand from mine. He stands and paces.

Then he sits back down and puts both hands on my face. "Listen. Here's how you know you can trust me. We'll go right now to Dentron for the pollen, and seeds and plants, and whatever we need to attempt to grow it on Zandia. We have the best ag experts there, I promise. The king's mate is human and an expert in agriculture. She's able to cultivate crops originally grown on Earth."

His voice is so low and persuasive. Honey and steel mixed. His eyes flash purple for a second. He sounds so sincere. "A token of my honesty, Kailani." He pauses. "I'll give you control of everything we collect." He twists to grab

46

the case of medicine and hands it to me. "It's yours, all right? Starting now."

I snatch it from his hands and clutch it to my chest, my heart pounding.

"All right? Do you trust me now?"

I squeeze the case so hard my fingers hurt. I don't trust him, but he just gave me the one gift I require for survival. The thing that my Kraa masters used to control me. He gave it freely. So I nod. "Yes." My breath comes fast and tight.

"Good. Listen, Kailani. The doctor on Zandia, Dr. Daneth, he's skilled. It's possible he can reverse the damage your owners did." He adds hastily, looking at my expression, "If you want him to try."

"I don't," I snap.

No more labs. Never again. I hate doctors.

He raises a hand. "On Zandia, we'll make you enough medicine to last your entire life."

"And all I have to do in return is…?" I raise my eyebrows.

Is it me or does he look slightly uncomfortable?

He clears his throat. "Become a contributing member of Zandian society."

"How? By mating a Zandian?"

His horns thicken and tilt in my direction, making my pulse pick up speed. Do they show his interest? His attraction to me? I know he wants me—I saw that thick erection tenting his leggings and tunic before.

He just shrugs and walks to the deck, staring out at the blackness. "In whatever way you choose."

It wouldn't matter if he were lying; I still have no other options, unless I plan to attack him once we're on Dentron and escape alone with the ship.

I weigh the idea for a few seconds—it would surely be

difficult to learn to captain this craft, but I think I could do it. Should I try once again to escape? I'd be my own master, in charge of my own destiny.

But for now, all I say is, "All right." I look down out the ports, at the receding lights, and the advancing ones. "Deal. Let's do this." First, I need the pollen. I'll figure out the rest later—once it's in my possession.

He jogs to his console to respond to a beeping signal and a red flashing light. Once it's resolved, he turns to me. "You need to sleep. Your body surely needs the rest."

We both look at the silver magna cuffs lying on the floor. He picks them up and tosses them into a cabinet. "Trust, right?" He looks at me for a long second then smiles. "Now that we have a deal, we don't need these."

My stomach flutters with arousal: Thinking about what he did when those cuffs were on is enough to make my body fill with that tingly, amazing feeling. I want to tell him, "What if we *want* them?"

But exhaustion takes over, and I yawn so widely that my face hurts.

"Trust." I yawn again. "Yes."

He grins. I swear he's thinking the same things I am—

"Maybe I will sleep." I barely get the words out before every muscle goes leaden with exhaustion. I slump back onto the bench, still clutching the case to my stomach. "Wake me when…" and I'm out.

KHRYS

She falls asleep mid-sentence as the collective events of the past hours hit her.

I carry her to a sleep bay and lie her on one of the bunks. I cover her with a blanket and adjust the medicine case, so it's not digging into her ribs. She's still holding it like it's the only *vecking* thing in the world that matters—and I suppose it is. A strand of hair falls into her face, and I push it back with my index finger.

"So soft," I whisper.

Her lashes brush her cheeks, and I resist the urge to kiss her lips while she slumbers.

Don't get too attached, I remind myself.

Now that she's asleep, I take the opportunity to slide a healing pack onto her arm. It will help balance her nutrition and give her healing medications, including a sleep aid that helps human bodies recover from trauma. Too bad it can't fix her headaches.

Too bad it can't fix my issues.

Reminded of my own concerns, I take a deep breath, check that Kailani is deeply asleep, and do the thing I dread. I put in a holo-call to my commander. I'd turned the comms off the moment I left Zandia to avoid communication, and I know I may face more serious consequences than a demotion for this.

"Master Seke, this is Captain Khrys." I keep my voice even. "Checking in from Starship A-25X, currently in Galaxy Ambi."

"Captain Khrys, you were not authorized for any mission." He doesn't waste words. He's seated at his workstation in the royal palace. Behind him stands his assistant and sergeant at arms, my friend Gabin.

"Forgive me, Master Seke, but I'm on my way back to Zandia. I secured a human bounty that will serve our planet well. Someone whose DNA may provide the answers to the Z4-A epidemic."

I glance toward the bunkroom. A feeling of guilt pierces

me, but I push it away. This is necessary. For Zandia. And to restore my honor. "I rescued a human female, Kailani. The engineered one who is stronger than normal and can fight off any human virus. She is intact. I will bring her back to King Zander and Dr. Daneth, so they may use her to understand human improvement and help our young."

"I have heard of no such human."

"She's very real. You can verify her stats. She made an escape before she went to auction, and I provided assistance."

"I see." Master Seke frowns.

"I've seen her strengths with my own eyes. She's better than her dossier suggests." I pause. "I have no doubts that everything reported about her is true."

Gabin pulls up Kailani's dossier and shares it with him. Master Seke's eyebrows rise into his smooth purple fore-head. "If that's true, Dr. Daneth will be very interested in studying her. Is it true she has enhanced anti-viral properties?"

"I have no way of verifying such a thing, but yes, that is what her former masters claimed."

I haven't asked her yet if it's true. My chest tightens, but I continue: "If she offers her unique attributes to benefit Zandia, I assume she will be granted a safe place to live?"

If I'd been able to buy her as I planned, this would be easier, but I didn't. Now she's an escaped slave, probably with an enormous bounty on her head. If she's caught by any being in the galaxy, her life could be forfeit. Probably not, considering her worth, but her fate likely would not be a life worth living.

"Where is she now?" Master Seke looks behind me, into the holo, as if seeking her. "I would like to hear her speak."

I stand and gesture toward the bunk room. "Sleeping with the aid of a med patch. She is relatively uninjured but has minor wounds and extreme exhaustion." I go and open the door, so he may observe her. I stare, too.

She's so lovely and small, huddled into herself in sleep. Her long black curls sprawl across the mattress. Her eyelids flutter—is she dreaming? She stirs and mumbles, readjusts her body, and falls back into deeper slumber.

I close the door and turn my attention back to my holo, where Seke is silent. "I'm sure she will be willing to speak to you once she is awake and healed."

Zandians don't lie, and those words—while I want to believe them—taste like ash in my mouth. Kailani may not present well to King Zander or Master Seke.

Even though I can't keep her, I may need to ensure she properly bonds to me as her master before we arrive. I can't risk her attacking another Zandian or acting wild. Nothing would be worse than if King Zander chose to return her to her owners instead of providing her with asylum.

Master Seke examines me over the holo.

I have no idea what he's about to say. He may tell me that I'm going to prison for life as soon as I return. He might tell me I'm banished. I hold my breath.

"Stand by." His voice is impersonal. "I will consult with the king."

It's only minutes, but it feels like hours before he blinks back into view. "I have reviewed the situation with King Zander. You are cleared to return with the human. As soon as you land, she will be taken into custody, as will you. At that time, King Zander will determine what comes next. Bringing her, of course, will help him tend to leniency."

I bow my head. "That is my hope, Master." Relief floods my body: So far, it's not automatic bad news for me.

Seke checks his wrist holo. "Excuse me." He moves away once again and leaves the room.

While Seke is conferring out of my earshot, Gabin looks left and right then steps into the holo. "You really got her?" His voice holds eager curiosity. "I remember you showing me the holo, and I thought you were out of your mind. Wasn't she at a high-security auction? Going for untold amounts of stein?" He's probably not supposed to speak to me, and I'm beyond glad to hear his voice. I still have one friend in this galaxy.

Pride swells in my chest. "Yes. I'd planned on offering Zandian crystal in exchange for her, but she made an escape attempt, and I went with it. Together we got out. That's how good her skills are." I think of how we worked together seamlessly.

"You took incredible risks." He shakes his head. "I'm glad you're safe."

I nod. "It paid off. How angry is the king with my disappearance?"

"Incandescent, but surely trending to forgiveness if you actually return with this human. You know he's a fair ruler. And some of the young are getting sicker." His face grows somber as he adds, "Especially the king's own heirs." He looks across the room. "I must go. Master Seke is coming." Gabin steps back and goes into his formal post of attention.

Master Seke, usually reticent, smiles and his voice holds excitement. "Dr. Daneth is eager to see if we can use any of her blood enhancements to help the young on Zandia beat this tricky virus. He is already preparing the testing equipment he will need. This could be a miracle for Zandia, Captain Khrys. For our king and for us all."

A spear of misgiving slashes through me. "He won't hurt her." It's as much a threat as a question.

Seke seems surprised. "You know he will not. All humans are valued. She will be treated with care and dignity as he examines her and removes blood and tissue samples for investigation."

I believe this to be true. I also am fairly sure that Kailani will not care for that distinction.

Master Seke looks at me evenly. "You are lucky that you are returning with such a prize. Please keep us updated on comms as to your progress. Once you hit atmosphere, we'll direct you."

"Understood. Thank you." I look back at her. "There is one more thing I need to do first to ensure her survival."

I explain to Master Seke about the medicine and her headaches. He approves the stop on Dentron and promises to send me all of Zandia's information on that planet, scant though it is.

"There are locals," he tells me, checking a holo doc. "Wild and clever although without tech. The weather is going to turn any time now with dangerous storms. Be careful. I've sent you maps enhanced with bio markers for plant matter— hopefully it will help you find the flower fields you need."

Master Seke signs off with a reminder to ensure the human is protected against any bacterial threats on Dentron, leaving me alone with my troubled thoughts...and the sleeping human.

I sigh and set the coordinates for Dentron. It's only two light years away; we'll be there in under an hour, even accounting for the detours I'll make around dangerous asteroid belts.

Kailani mutters and cries out, and I hurry to the bunkroom, leaving the ship on auto-pilot.

"Shhh," I soothe, sitting on the cot beside her and stroking her cheek. "You're safe." I lie on the cot beside her to pull her into my arms. "No more headaches, little warrior. Never again. I promise."

Whether she can hear me or not is a mystery, but the instant I hold her, she murmurs something unintelligible and relaxes into my grasp. Her breathing evens. And although it's folly and will only lend me a false sense of intimacy, I continue to hold her while she slumbers.

"Everything will be all right," I say, even though it's not likely—for her or for myself.

I try not to think about how right she feels in my embrace because the second we get to Zandia and she finds out about my omission, she's going to hate me forever.

I just don't see any other solution.

CHAPTER 5

*K*ailani

I awaken with a start and a guttural cry, completely confused.

"Careful...easy, little warrior." A deep voice sounds in my ear. "You're safe. We're nearing Dentron."

"What?" I push at his arms, panic suffusing my nerves. Then, "Oh." I'm lying on a cot with his much larger body wrapped around mine. His massive chest flexes under my palms. He smells faintly of rich spice and citrus and delicious male.

I breathe in his scent as it all comes back: The auction. The escape. How Khrys touched me and brought me untold pleasure. Heat pulses between my legs at the memory. Or perhaps it's from the feel of his hard body against my softer one. I realize I'm running my hands over his pecs, freely exploring the chiseled lines of muscle, and I freeze.

"How long was I asleep?" I stretch, expecting to feel pain from our escape or even a twinge in my ass from his spanking, but everything is completely back to normal. My body feels as strong and limber as always.

For a moment, panic returns and my hands fly to check, but I find the case with my medicine is still there. I open it and take out the dropper, still half-expecting Khrys to suddenly take it away from me or deny me my full dosage.

He just watches in silence, then gets up from the bed and offers his hand, as if I'm some delicate creature who requires his assistance getting out of bed. I want to sneer over it, but the fact is, no being has ever shown me any consideration, and I can't deny the warm tingles it produces everywhere.

I take his hand and climb out of bed, looking around at the small bunk room. Did we sleep together? All night? Even though I know nothing happened, the thought makes my heart beat faster.

"There's a washtube in the washroom. Do you know how to use one?"

I shake my head.

"Come, I'll show you."

He takes me to the facility and presses a button. A pneumatic door of a cylindrical chamber slides open. He nudges me inside, and I jerk back and resist, suddenly afraid of whatever it is he's trying to do to me.

"Easy, little warrior. It's just for washing—it's not a prison." He steps back to let me retreat from it. "Here, I'll go first." He steps into the cylinder. "You'll remove your clothing and step in. This button activates washing." He points at a button on the inside wall. "The tube door will close, and the cylinder fills with water and soap, then empties, rinses you and blows warm air to dry your skin."

My stomach is still drawn up tight in defense mode. It could be some kind of trick. I've never seen such a device before.

Khrys glances at me and must see I still don't trust him. His horns lift and tilt apart from each other. He frowns and steps out. I quickly dart backward. His frown deepens. "Kailani, watch me," he commands.

He pulls his white tunic off his head. I swallow, eye-to-chest with his massive bare trunk, powerful and muscled. A peachy-purple map of ridges and valleys. He holds my gaze steadily as he toes off his boots, then tucks his thumbs in the waistband of his leggings and peels them down and off. He has no underclothing beneath them, and his semi-hard cock springs out and bobs.

I try to swallow but fail. When I lift my gaze from his malehood, he's still staring directly at me. His brown irises seem to have deepened to violet. His horns have thickened and lean my way. "It's like this," he says, stepping backward into the shower, without removing his steady gaze from mine.

My nipples tighten beneath the clothing he provided me. The curious warmth he incited yesterday after my punishment returns—heat coiling in my low belly, between my legs.

I don't mean to, but somehow, I find myself stepping forward, as if magnetically drawn to his body when he moves away. He continues to hold me captive with his intense gaze. Out of my periphery, I see his cock grow stiffer, pointing at me while he presses the button on the shower wall.

The door slides shut, and he's blocked from my view. I draw in several deep steadying breaths as the sound of water pouring into the small tube fills my ears. The washroom grows steamy.

There's nothing to see anymore—the door is closed—and yet, I remain standing in the same place, staring at the wash-tube as if I might see through its walls and watch the giant warrior bathe.

Does he find it pleasurable? The water must be warm, considering how the room has steamed up. Something changes, and the water stops flowing. A gurgling sound indicates the water draining. A citrus-spice scent fills the room—must be the soap. I hear motors come to life—the air blowers he referred to. Then the pneumatic door slips open. Even though I just saw him naked a moment ago, the gorgeous spectacle hits me full-force again. Huge, muscular purple male invades every sense. His thickened horns and cock both point toward me like I'm their compass home.

I dart forward to pick up his leggings and hand them to him like a house-slave because I'm far too affected by the sight than I want to be.

"Ready to try?" he rumbles.

Try...? All I can think of is his cock. Am I ready to try sex? Ready to try him. Ready to ride that huge, thick member.

But then I realize... he must mean the washtube.

"Oh! Um, yes." I bob my head. "Yes, I'll try now. Thank you." I sound breathless.

He steps into his leggings and picks up his tunic but doesn't put it on. He also doesn't leave.

"I, um, don't need help," I say in a rush. "I think I understand now."

He inclines his head and walks out of the washroom, closing the door behind him. I feel the loss of him everywhere. I even step toward the door as if to follow—to call back to him and say, actually, could he show me the washtube again? Or maybe, step into it with me and wash me with those huge purple hands of his?

I shake my head to clear the thoughts and strip out of my clothing. In the washtube, I press the button as he indicated. Water rushes in from all sides—so must faster than I expected. I bite back a shriek of surprise. The water is warm, extremely pleasant, just vigorous. It massages my body in a dozen places with the hard streams. The washtube fills rapidly. In a moment it's up to my waist. Then my shoulders. Will it stop?

I tip my head up toward the ceiling, suddenly terrified of drowning. I draw a deep breath before it covers my head! I open my eyes and the soap stings them. I squeeze them shut again. Just as my panic begins to surge, the water level drops away, draining as rapidly as it rose.

The citrusy smell fills my nostrils, making me think of Khrys, even though it will be me, now, who smells this way, too. Thinner streams of water spray my body, rinsing the soap from it, and then the warm air blows fast and hard, drying every drop.

The door automatically opens, and I find myself reluctant to step out. Sorry it's over. Now that I know how it works, I want to do it again. I've had very few moments in my life where my body experienced pleasure. One of them was last night when Khrys brought me to orgasm.

This morning, waking in his arms.

Now this.

All the experiences were new and therefore somewhat stressful, so I only half-enjoyed them.

This one I can simply repeat with the press of a button. But would it be wasteful? Would Khrys reprimand me?

The thought of his reprimand makes my inner thighs squeeze together. Maybe I want a repeat of that experience as well.

I push the button again, an unfamiliar smile curving my lips as the cycle begins again.

~

KHRYS

. . .

Aw, *veck*. I lean my forehead against the door to the washroom and squeeze my throbbing member.

The way the little warrior looked at me after I stepped out of the shower still has me hard. She eyed my cock like she wanted to know how it tasted. What it felt like to ride it fast and hard. Her fear of the washtube had dropped away and desire simmered there beneath it.

I'd scented her arousal. I know the intoxicating smell now, after last night. Like warm honey cakes and Zandian starshine.

When I hear her restart the washtube, I groan. The thought of her in there, naked.

Oh stars, she's so beautiful!

I want her. Badly.

But she's not mine. Her purpose on Zandia is far higher than mating and breeding. She could be the answer to the Z4-A epidemic affecting the youngest generation. She is way too important. And considering how low I've fallen with King Zander, I can't imagine he would grant any petition I made to mate her.

Still, I must win her trust. Bond her to me for the time being in order to bring her in willingly. Her existence up until now has been horrible. I know with certainty Zandia will be far more pleasant, but she doesn't know that yet.

Hopefully my giving her control of her medicine and going to retrieve the flowers necessary to make more will be enough to secure her confidence in me and my species.

I squeeze my cock again, through my leggings. Down, boy. Claiming her would be wrong. I don't want to lead her to believe I can mate her when there's a possibility I will end up in the dungeons for this stunt.

Of course, I'm hoping that won't be the case. I'm hoping this restores my honor, but it could go the other way.

I force myself away from the washroom door and back to the controls. It must be nearly time to land the ship.

Kailani

AFTER MY SHOWER, I find a comb in the washroom and brush my hair. I look in the glass, feeling, for the first time in my life, beautiful. Whether it's from pampering my body in the washtube or the way the Zandian looks at me, I can't be sure. All I know is the feeling isn't unpleasant.

My whole life, this body has been a Kraa tool. Something to cut and carve and change. Something to be used for their purposes.

They had no interest in my beauty. I wasn't for breeding. I can't compare my existence with that of breeding slaves. I don't know whether theirs is easier or harder. All I know is sexuality was missing from my life until the previous planet rotation.

Until Khrys.

I suddenly don't hate my body the way I used to. In fact, I almost… like it.

The ship dips and rumbles, and I realize we're landing. I step out of the washroom to stand behind Khrys and look through the port windows. I press my face up against the glass. It's so thick that there's no temperature gradient from outside. The material gives the same warmth as the air around me.

"It's dark."

He nods. "We're in an uninhabited field, cloaked. We're safe. First light comes soon. You will recognize the flowers?"

"Yes." At least I hope so.

"Then you will come with me. It may take both of us searching to find them. You should ready yourself and eat something first."

"Oh." My stomach lurches, and I glance back at the bench —my case is still there. "Good." I hurry back to touch it. I've never had a young, but I imagine this is how a mother feels when she can't let it out of her sight.

"It's cold and might rain; you'll need this jacket." He hands me a sleek garment with a hood. "It's weather resistant. Remember that the air is thinner than your old planet, so you may feel a little out of breath at first."

I put the jacket beside the case while I use the ship's washroom and eat a packet of food. "My lungs are more powerful than a regular human's."

He nods. "I know."

Excitement starts to grow. Dangerous or not, this is an adventure—my first, ever. "I get to walk around without the Kraa masters." My voice must hold extreme excitement.

"What?" He turns from the console where he's reading some holo docs.

"I could never walk freely on the planet." I shake my head. "I spent most of my time in a lab or sometimes in a small outdoor barred yard with the other humans for a little exercise."

He looks pained, so I add, "But that's behind me now."

"Yes." He looks away. "We need to be careful. Seke sent, —ah, I looked up all the information I could find on Dentron." He clears his throat. "Like you mentioned, the locals are not advanced—they're feral and kill strangers on sight. They use poisoned arrows that can travel over half a mile. But I've found a field far from their listed habitations. Hopefully it has the flowers."

"Okay." I'm about to ask who or what a *Seke* is, when pale streaks of light begin to wind across the alien sky, fingers of cerulean and pink against the inky black. Without warning, several suns radiate light, as if turned on by an invisible giant.

"Oh!" I gasp. "It's beautiful—I've never seen anything like it."

"You're going to love Zandia." His face breaks out into a smile, and it seems like he's focusing on something very distant. "We have gorgeous sunsets. And there's a waterfall with a crystal grotto. When the lights shine, it's just…" he shakes his head, seemingly at a loss for words. "The crystals are powerful and healing—at least to my species. But I think certain humans also find them so."

"I'd like to see a waterfall."

"You will."

"Beings can just go there, to see it? Do you need permission?" I'm trying to understand.

"It's open to all Zandians."

"Could I go with you? Will you take me there when we arrive? I would love to see it."

His smile dips. "I will take you there as soon as I can. Right now let's focus on the mission." He gets up and retrieves something from a cabinet. Rips open a packet.

My senses are on high alert as I scent the tang of medicinal alcohol, the refined blend that is used to ensure human inoculation kits are germ-free. Before I recognize my actions, I've snarled out a low growl and stand in attack mode, heart pounding.

"What are you doing?" My voice is fierce even as adrenaline makes me sick with anxiety. "What's in your hand?"

The thing, long and slim, glints in the light. I back up.

"Stars, Kailani." He looks at me with concern. I note that

he, too, now stands at attention, ready to parry or attack. "It's an inoculation for you. To protect against bacterial infections you could get on the planet. There's a kind of insect here that carried a bacterium which—" He breaks off when I start to hyperventilate.

"No." I shake my head vigorously. I may be enhanced, but my capability for fear seems to only be heightened. The last needle that slid under my skin was to prepare me for a procedure that comes back to me in nightmares. I breathe faster.

"*Veck.*" He puts the needle down.

The clink it makes on the surface of his console makes me shudder in fresh horror as the memories of the Kraa flash up in full color. A strange, staccato sound fills the space ship. I realize it's me—hiccuping for air. I sit and wrap my arms around myself, my chest heaving.

Khrys appears in front of me. "Kailani!" He lifts me and pulls me into his arms. "Easy, little warrior." He touches my pulse, my neck, my face. "You're okay. Everything is all right."

I can't stop the violent shaking in my limbs. "No," I contradict him.

"Speak to me. What's wrong?"

I suck in air. The world is full of static. The feel of his warm hands grounds me, and I swim back to reality. I tremble and lean into his body, trying to forget every last image in my mind.

After a few seconds, I force myself to take a slow breath. "I'm fine now." Although the feel of his body is fortifying, I sit up straight. "I don't want to talk about it."

"We can't get those flowers until you do." His voice is kind but firm. "I lost you for a moment. I need to understand what happened."

His arms are gentle around me as I process my emotions. I need those flowers; therefore, I must comply with his request. If I think of it in a dispassionate way I can tell him.

"Every inoculation I've ever received was a muscular numbing agent." I don't look at his face. Instead, I stare out at the flickers of color outside the port window. "The Kraa often did enhancements on me while I was paraylzed but not asleep. They didn't care if I felt pain because they needed me to be alert, so they could check my brain activity to see if their procedures were successful. If I'd been a good slave recently, they might add a bit of a numbing agent, but not much."

I bite my lip. "When I saw the needle, it brought me right back there. My mind knew it was different, but my body didn't." My voice breaks. The panic grows again, so I take a deep breath, then another.

"I did not know." His voice seems full of pain. "I am sorry."

I point across the room. "I'm strong enough. I can withstand any human virus, anyway. I don't need it." I blink. "Please, put it out of my sight. I'll be fine on the planet. It was a momentary panic. That is all."

"Kailani." He sighs. "The bacteria on this planet are different from a virus. They can still make you very ill. I'm immune to it, but if I brought it back, I could kill you."

CHAPTER 6

 *hrys*

VECK. This complication, unexpected and intense, could prevent us from getting her flower supply before I need to get her back to Zandia. This detour alone—which may take over a solar rotation, will waste precious time in which the halflings back on Zandia get sicker. We simply don't have time to wait even more time for her to master her panic.

But beyond that, seeing her in such distress affects me physically. Now I understand why they say humans bring out emotions in my normally stoic species. The need for me to protect her from her pain overwhelms me.

I sit on the bench and pull her down onto my lap.

"You're stronger than you think." I turn her, so I can look into her face. "You can do this."

"I—I really don't think I can." She shakes her head. Her whole demeanor is downcast and tense.

"You've survived this long." I touch her cheek. "I know

you can handle one inoculation more because you're strong. You helped us escape. You're brilliant. You've got perseverance and bravery."

She blinks, her eyes wide. "Wow. Do you really mean those things?"

"Has no being told you this before?" I curse the universe for putting this incredible human into such a horrible situation.

"I'm appreciated by the Kraa for my functionality. Not for myself." She frowns. "I am a tool to them. I just inconveniently happen to be alive with thoughts and feelings."

If I could, I'd kill every last Kraa that exists just to give her a sense of closure. "I meant every word." I pause and choose my next words with care. "What if you sit here, just like this, and I give you the inoculation? You can tell me when to do it. Or you could even give it to yourself."

She shivers but doesn't say no. She looks again to the window, and I know what she's thinking.

"The weather is going to turn. If we don't get the flowers soon, the rains will come and ruin the pollen for this season. We have a very short window of opportunity."

She sighs and looks back at me. "All right. You do it."

"Good." I fetch the device from the console.

Her whole body goes still as I take her back into my arms.

"I can't look." She clears her throat and taps her food rapidly on the smooth floor of the cabin.

"I'm readying it now. It will make a noise, and you'll smell the alcohol, but I won't touch it to your skin until you say *yes*."

I flip the protective cap up, and she flinches, hard, so hard her whole body jerks into mine with force.

I steady her. "It won't hurt—not even for a human. When I receive inoculations, I feel the briefest pin prick, and a cold sensation as the medicine goes into the tissue. It will only take a millisecond."

"All right." She nods and squeezes her eyes shut. She takes a deep breath. "Do it."

In a flash, I press the sleek cylinder to her arm and press the trigger. There's a short click, and it's done.

She sits so still, I can't tell if she's passed out or not. Then she says, "Is that all?"

I put the spent device behind me. "All over."

"That was it?" She opens her eyes. Touches her arm. "It doesn't hurt." She looks up at me, and her eyes fill with tears. "You didn't lie." She gulps. "I'm all right. There's no surgery."

Suddenly, she burst into sobs, her shoulders heaving with cries so deep and long that I grab her again.

"I can't believe I'm not in that cell," she sniffs between jerks of her body. "Owned by the Kraa. It's all I've wanted for so long, and now that I'm out…" She squeezes herself against me, like she's trying to merge with my skin. "I don't even know how to do this. To live in a new environment."

"You'll figure it out." I stroke her hair. "You don't need to do it all at once."

"I can't go back into captivity and have them experiment on me whenever they want. I just can't. The possibility that I could—it's almost worse than being free. It's so terrifying."

"You're safe now." I hold her until she cries it out.

The suns rise higher in the sky, and dual beams of light stream in from opposite directions, casting an intricate shadow pattern across our bodies.

She looks up at me and swipes a hand across her eyes. There's peace there and a new determination. She is back in charge of herself again.

"I'm ready. Tell me what I need to do."

Kailani

"Stay ten paces behind me," he whispers. "Walk in my footsteps."

"Got it." I'm much shorter than he is, but my stride is long because I use my enhanced muscles to leap from spot to spot where he's crushed down the crispy waist-high grasses with his large boots.

"Your breathing okay?" He keeps the same pace as the sky gradually picks up more color, reds shooting through the original blue and pink. There are clouds, too, the kind that burst with moisture. So far it's been dry, which is good news. We can get the flowers while they're intact.

"Fine. Yes." It took a few minutes of deep gulps of air, but my strong lungs adjusted even faster than his Zandian ones.

"I'm great." The cold air on my cheeks exhilarates me. Even the thoughts of dangerous locals can't dampen my boundless joy at just walking around without Kraa slave masters watching my every move. And having mastered that inoculation with his help? It made me feel invincible. I did a thing that was in my worst nightmares—and I survived.

"I've downloaded an ag map of the territory onto my holo. We'll walk a mile due Southeast, and we should hit a field where we might find flowers." He turns to look at me.

"How did you get such a map?" I leap across a boggy patch of grass, black mud seeping up between thick gray roots.

"Zandians have information about many planets in the galaxies." His shoulders seem stiff. I feel like his voice is different from before, almost like he's hiding something from me.

Suddenly, I hear something. On instinct, I grab his sleeve. "Footsteps to the left. Get down."

I immediately dive and nestle into the grass. He's beside me in a flash, his head inches from mine. It's not the time or place, but the warmth from his body and his lips so close remind me of what we did on the ship, when he spanked me and brought me pleasure.

"You heard that even before I did." His voice holds grudging admiration. "Good work."

"Cochlear surgery when I was eight solar cycles. I can't tell if it's sentients or animals." I suppress my surge of pride at his praise. Speaking of the surgery doesn't bring quite the rush of horror as usual—whether it's his presence or the fact that I was able to take a vaccine voluntarily, I'm more in control of my emotions.

He cocks his head. "I think they're four-legged. I'm going to check. Stay down." He hovers his hand over my back and gets into a quick crouch, so nimbly that I raise my eyebrows. He peers above the tall grasses. "It's a kind of antlex, a herd of ten."

He examines the horizon in all directions. "There are a few herds around us. They should be harmless—herbivores. Placid."

He gets up and reaches a hand down for me.

"Thank you." I smile as I stand and look around. I've never seen a wild animal before. The grazing beasts are striped brown and white, colors that blend into the landscape. Their horns are impossibly curled, corkscrew twists that glint amber in the light. They're spectacular to me. "We're safe."

"It seems so," he says, but frowns. He examines the distance again and blinks. "I don't see anything else." He hesitates, as if something is bothering him. He looks up at the sky, where the previous gorgeous pinks and oranges have been obscured by thick gray clouds, long like blankets. "Let's keep going before the weather changes."

He's moving fast again, almost jogging, and despite my much shorter legs, I keep up effortlessly, thanks to years of muscle fiber enhancement drug therapy.

In a minute, we near a small patch of scraggly trees, almost like a wind-line, and beyond that is a vast field of flowers. A few of them, smaller but no less gorgeous, grow amongst the trees. All of the flowers are blue, but my eyes zero in on the ones that I remember: These are the ones I need —I recognize them.

I catch my breath. "They're really here."

The relief I feel is almost unbearable. "We can get them." My voice catches. I crouch down and reach out, touching the nearest one. With these, I can survive without the Kraa. "I can get them." The petals are soft and springy, and my finger glides softly down the stem. "Look, Khrys. See how this one has a slight sheen on it?" I touch it lightly. "This is the one." I point to the flower next to it. "This one is darker, just a bit. It doesn't have the right pollen."

He looks intently, bends down to examine it, too. "Got it."

I smell the flower. "It's like life incarnate." I close my eyes for a second.

"Don't let your guard down now," Khrys warns. He's back on his feet, and his stance is that of a warrior, peering around. "Work fast. I have a bad feeling about this place."

"We're alone, except for the antlex. Right?" It's beautiful and empty, even with the darkening skies, just us and some far off animals and the rolling fields, miles of them, as far as the eye can see. There's a closer herd of antlex, too. Their musky odor drifts over on the breeze, mixing with the fresh scent of the fields.

"Why do you have a bad feeling?" He is a warrior, after

all. I should pay attention to his intuition. I stand up and check the area, but I don't see or hear anything unusual.

"It seems too easy." He lowers his voice. "I'm not used to simple situations. But the only thing around is the beasts." He shakes his head. "Keep an eye out while you work."

I slide the first canvas bag off my shoulder, pull on the gloves, and remove the shears. Holding them in my gloved hand, I bend down. "Get as many as you can," I urge, but he's already busy and has half a bag filled.

The stalks are thick and reedy, but the sharp blades cut them like water. The pale blue blossoms are heavy with thick yellow pollen. On the ripest plants, the heads hang low, weighed down by their golden treasure.

"So many," I whisper, piling flower after flower into my bag. On a whim, I taste some pollen, wondering if extra doses can keep me headache-free longer. It's got a neutral taste, but is oddly appealing, so I eat more. Then I stuff some flowers into the pocket of my jacket, just in case I need them later. I feel the urgent need to have them on my person at all times.

"On Zandia, we have ag experts who can figure out how to make these grow." Khrys looks at me. "Humans, Kailani." He's digging up a few by the roots and placing them into storage bags with root support.

"Slaves?"

"Not slaves. Humans must have a Zandian sponsor—a master, if you will, and they must be contributing members of society, but they are free. I told you that."

"Free but with masters."

"Yes. Usually their mate."

Mate. I dart a look at him, heat suddenly swirling between my legs.

Would he be my mate? My sponsor?

My...master? I hated the word before now, but remembering the way he corrected me on the ship, I might not find such a master so unappealing.

I sneak a glance at his impossibly large hands. The way his horns tilt and lean in my direction when he catches me looking. His nostrils flare like he catches my scent, and I flush, realizing, suddenly, what he must smell.

My arousal. I'm wet for him. What would it be like to breed with such a male? I've never thought of such a thing without shuddering, but now, I find myself suddenly quite interested.

I give my head a shake. *Focus, Kailani.* We have flowers to pick.

My hands blur as I gather as many flowers as I can, stuffing the bag until it's overfull, and I have to push the flowers down to close the water-tight seam. Then I start on filling my next sack.

"I'm getting the dried seeds, too." He snips some withered blooms and shakes them into another container.

The sky rumbles. A sudden mist descends, patchy fog, thicker in some areas, swirling like smoke. "*Veck*, this weather is odd. We need to go soon. Let's finish." Khrys's voice is taut.

I glance upward. The clouds have darkened and seem lower. Is the air thicker?

"I think it's going to storm right now," I whisper. "The pressure is changing fast. I feel it in my body." I touch my ears and my chest.

Khrys nods. He says something, but it's drowned out by a louder crash from the sky, like boulders tumbling down a metal chute. The closest antlex tense up; one flicks its tail, and another goes silent, head to the side. Without warning, I feel the unease that Krys seemed to sense before, but I can't tell why—

Suddenly Khrys's horns shoot up. "Kailani!" His voice is sharp. "Get down. *Now.*"

He grabs me and tugs my arm hard, and I crash down beside him into the packed earth, crushing flowers beneath my body. Something whirs over my head, and the flower beside me is sliced clean from the stalk. By an arrow.

"We're not alone. The locals have found us."

My breath comes fast and my cheek presses into the dirt and rough detritus of old stems and leaves, dried out and scratchy. The scent of the crushed leaves and blossoms, green and woodsy, rises. "Where?"

"Straight out. And behind us. They've encircled us. *Veck.* They must have used the herds of antlex as a cover."

"And now that they're attacking, the animals are scared." I put my hand out and touch the sack. "We have to get away."

"Here." Khrys grapples at his waist and slides something to me. "It's a laser gun. I've set it to high stun. Use it when you have to."

He doesn't even hesitate. The fact that he trusts me with an actual weapon—something I could turn on him instead and kill him—fills me with such gratitude and emotion that I can't focus on the danger for a second.

He has another one, and he adjusts something on the handle. "We're going to fight our way out of this."

I bite my lip, forgetting about my surge of feelings—all that exists now is our escape. "When?"

"Soon." His voice is terse. "Wait for my command."

I scan the area, but see nothing. "Where?" I can't believe my enhanced eyes can't find them. The mist plays tricks, showing me figures where there are none, hiding the real beings. "I don't see." My body begins to tremble with fear and frustration. "Why don't I see them? With my eyes, I should."

"They're in camouflage." He sounds disgusted with himself. "I should have seen it. Point it at a being's chest and pull the trigger. Don't flinch. The laser sight will show you when you're locked on."

"I still can't—"

The grass around me erupts into motion. The closest patch of flowers rises and moves toward me, with arms and legs and a face. I scream. I can't understand what's happening, and before I realize that it's a being in a cleverly created suit of foliage, an arrow flies at my face—

"Move!" Khrys grabs me and jerks. My arm explodes in pain from the tug but the arrow zings harmlessly past me, so close to my ear that I feel the barest brush of the feather tail. "Fire, Kailani. Now."

I raise the weapon. I force myself to focus and get into the zone of attack that helped me so well back at the auction. When the world slows to a crawl, I know I've hit the sweet spot. A local being pops up out of the mist and raises a bow to his shoulder; my weapon is ready first, and I fire, dropping the being to the ground. Then I get another one.

Behind me, Khrys roars a fearsome cry and shoots fast, dropping at least five. "There are so many of them," he calls out. "At least forty. Our only option is to scare them into retreat."

So far, the locals haven't faltered. A flock of arrows fly, singing in the air with high, wheedling screams. I duck and whirl, using my enhanced vision to predict where they'll be when they hit me, and barely avoid the attack.

"Don't even touch the arrow tip on the ground," Khrys orders. "I don't know how much toxin is fatal to us."

He shoots off his laser guns. Ragged cries and screams arise from the locals as a body falls hard.

When Khrys fires again, the mood of the locals changes.

They roar as one, the voices merging into a symphony of sound, swelling like the thunder in the sky. Then they run toward us, arrows coming like hail.

"Leave the sacks and run," Khrys orders, grabbing my free hand.

My heart rips in half at his command, but I'm already running with him, as fast as we can, even harder than we did back at the auction—in the opposite direction of our craft.

Landscape skims by, the flower field recedes. We're going so fast that the arrows stop; I can only assume that the locals are focused on running, not shooting at moving targets buried in mist. But their footsteps never waver, and they seem to be closing the gap. "They're gaining on us," I pant, and the panic spurs us both into a new burst of speed.

But as at the auction, I can only do this for so long. I start to feel desperation, when we see something new through the fog—craggy foothills dotted with twisted trees.

"Finally," Khrys rasps, pulling me behind the closest trunk. We're panting, and I can barely breathe. "When they get closer, we attack. Our weapons are deadlier. All we need is this cover, and we can drop them all."

Dizzy with exhaustion, I drop to a crouch and grab my head, trying to control my air. "Understood."

"They're fanning out. But we've got the higher ground." Khyrs' voice is clear and precise. "On my command, you attack to your right. I go left."

"Yes," I gasp. I stand up and ready my weapon. In the near distance, figures waver and get into formation.

But suddenly, everything changes. With a particularly loud eruption, the clouds open up and dump freezing rain. The beings in front of us immediately break ranks and turn to each other, then—to my amazement and relief—turn around.

"The locals are turning back!" Khry's voice lifts with exuberance. "They're going the other way."

Indeed, the entire group of them races in the direction we came. In the distance, a herd of antlex scream and rear up and gallop to the left, disappearing over a ridge.

"Khrys?" I blink against the rain, which has a biting urgency against my face. "Why would they all run away from a little rain?" I wipe my brow and shiver—the liquid is so cold it's like ice. "Even the animals?"

"I don't know." His voice is tense. "Perhaps the rain is a sign of worse weather to come. I suggest we find shelter."

As he speaks, the raindrops increase—now they are the size of eyeballs. The protective gear keeps me dry enough, but I feel the power of the water through the fabric, and the sheer amount of rain is blinding. "This way." I point ahead. "Higher ground, and it's rock. Maybe we can find a cave."

We scramble up the hill for what seems like forever, as the visibility worsens. "Faster," urges Khrys.

I'm still out of breath from our run, and my energy flags. It's all I can do to drag myself up the next part of the slope by grabbing a thick root and pulling, inch by excruciating inch.

"You got it." Khrys grabs my hand to help.

Then the hail starts. At first, the individual crystals are tiny and thin like paper. Within seconds, they've grown bigger than my pinkie nail, each icy shard has sharp claws.

A particularly hard hail punctures my jacket and the skin on my arm, freeing red blood that immediately turns pink with dilution and runs to the ground. "The gear is not holding up! We need safety!" I gasp.

"*Veck*, this storm will kill us," mutters Khrys. "I've never seen hail like this." He pulls me to his body and shields my head with his arms, scanning our surroundings. "Come on, I think I see a cave." He keeps me sheltered under his arm and guides me further up the slope. He was right—after a harrowing few moments, we're nestled into a cavity in the rocks. The cave goes deep into the cliff and has a thick over-hang at the entrance.

"Back here, away from the wind." He pulls me further back into the cave to the dry dust out of reach of the swirling nightmare outside.

"Whew." I collapse to the ground, breathing hard. The cave smells like dirt but nothing else; thankfully, we're the only beings using it for shelter.

"We're safe from the ice balls." Khrys points. They're now the size of my fist with wicked spikes. They slam into the ground and shatter into ice fragments, sometimes piercing an inch or two deep into the soil before breaking apart.

"Stars, this storm is more powerful than most weapons." Khrys turns to me. "Are you hurt? Take off the jacket, so I can see." He helps me peel off the garment. "The tunic, too. You're soaked."

The circumstances prevent me from any shyness; all I want is to be safe. Still, being half naked in front of him sets erotic images free in my mind. My nipples peak in the cold air, and my cheeks flush.

Khrys takes my arm. Now that we're out of the down-pour, the blood is more evident. "We need to wrap this."

"It's just a scratch. I can't even feel pain." I look with curiosity at the wound, then at him. "Are you all right?"

"Yes." His voice is hoarse. I think he's looking at my nipples, but then he turns away. "My skin is thicker than yours. The hail didn't hurt me." He removes his shoulder satchel. "I have a few emergency supplies." He pulls out a cloth which he wraps around my cut. "There. That should close the wound."

"Thank you." I blink at the white wrap, trying to process

what's happening. How *much* has happened since the Kraa brought me to the auction.

The thunder roars and crackles, and the ground reverberates with the sound, the tremors going into my body and shaking my skull. "This storm is so violent."

At the bottom of the hill, the dried grass turns to a churning river as water collects into a channel and hurtles past, tumbling boulders effortlessly. Hail shimmers like glass ornaments, bobbing by the thousands.

"That would kill us faster than the arrows." I shudder from the sudden panic and the chill and the exhaustion. And the cold. I realize that the temperature has dropped.

"We're high enough that we should stay above the water line. *I hope*," he adds. He takes off his coat, reaches back into his pack and unwraps a silver heat blanket.

"Take off your clothes. All of them." He looks at me through the dimness of the cave where the blanket catches what little light enters from the gloomy wilderness outside. "We need to let them dry. You humans are prone to hypothermia."

"I…" It might be the shock of the situation, but I don't move.

He drops the blanket and comes to my side. "Your breeches are soaked. They'll prevent you from warming your core temperature."

He grabs the sturdy material and tugs it down my wet hips. The fabric sticks, and when he inserts his strong hands between my thighs to coax the pants down, his knuckles brush up against my panties.

I suck in my breath. "Oh."

He looks up at me, and his eyes flash. His horns stiffen. For a second, I think he's going to touch me again, but he looks away and tugs my garment down, only stopping when they hit the top of my boots.

"The boots." He laughs. "I forgot these."

He swings me into his arms and suddenly deposits me on a flat boulder that's at the height of his chest. "Sit here for a second, little warrior."

He removes my boots and places them aside—and then the breeches are easy to slide off my ankles.

"Use this until I make a fire." He wraps the silver thermoblanket around my shoulders and tucks it around my body. His hands linger just a moment as he arranges it, and he slides one hand softly over my thigh.

Already I feel better—he was right about the wet clothes making me colder. I clutch the blanket tightly to my chest with criss-crossed fists.

"I have a few nutrition tubes for you. Start with this and see if you want more." He hands me one full of a gel that I suck down eagerly.

"You don't need it?" I recall that I haven't seen him eat anything in the time we've been together.

"Zandians require the crystalline energy of our planet for survival. We eat only once every ten planet rotations."

I shake my head at the second tube. "I'm good for now. Thank you."

He touches my leg softly through the blanket, his fingers lingering. "Good." His eyes meet mine, and he smiles.

A slow burn works its way from the point of contact, his fingers on my body, up to my core. He places his palm onto my leg, possessive.

"Khrys?" My voice comes out husky. I shift my thighs.

He steps back.

"I'll lay your clothing out on these rocks at the back of the cave," he says, taking an armful of sodden cloth into the darkness. "There are dry branches back here we can use for a fire. That will help."

I'm glad to hear it, but my eyes adjust fast. When I see him start to strip, my heart pounds a little harder. This Zandian has a magnificent body, and I can't deny the effect he has on me, even in these circumstances.

When he comes back with thick pieces of wood shedding bark and dust, he works fast: Using something from his shoulder bag, he has a fire going not too far from the front of the cave entrance.

"And now we'll warm up." He stands in front of me, all chiseled muscles lit up from the flickering of the fire. He lifts me from the rock and settles us down together a few feet from the flames.

"Come." He pulls me into his lap and rearranges the blanket to cover us both like a tent. "We need to warm up."

Outside our cave, the storm gathers force as we huddle together, our bodies warming little by little. The rain and hail together are a fearsome combination, but thank stars, they're falling straight down.

"If wind blew that into our cave, I don't know what would happen." I nestle into Khrys' arms, craving the comfort he brings.

A twig snaps and sends up a shower of sparks, and the warmth from the fire and his body soothe me.

"We got lucky." He wraps his arms around me.

His strong, muscular arms with his smooth purple skin.

Naked purple skin.

Entirely naked.

I feel his hard cock push into my backside, and the urgent need between my thighs grows stronger. I make a small moan in my throat and push myself into his body. With intent.

"We are lucky, aren't we?" I run my hand along his thigh.

My heart races with nerves and arousal. I'm being so bold, so forward. Surely it isn't my place to offer myself like this? All I know is that my body craves him, and I don't have the power to resist.

He growls and bites my neck. "Ah, Kailani, you're driving me crazy." His voice is a low rumble. His cock is even harder now. I know he wants me, too.

"Show me how crazy." I twist myself around and look up at his face. "Khrys."

He laughs. "Be careful what you ask for, little warrior."

"Do you think I can't handle it?"

"Well, let's see." He raises a brow. "Do you want to find out?"

My gut lurches in anticipation. "Maybe I do."

My eyes flicker and shut. I can still half-way see the flames waxing and waning against my eyelids. They match the desire that pulses through my veins. "Hmmm."

I shriek in delighted surprise as he scoops me up and stands, maneuvering me with no effort at all.

"Let's start with something like this, shall we?"

He places me back onto the rock, the same one from before, and pulls the silver blanket from my body. I'm naked except for the strip of fabric covering my pussy. I'm not cold anymore, but my nipples pebble under his gaze.

"How remiss I am. I never removed your panties. We need those to dry out as well."

His eyes flash in the firelight as he props me up with one arm and tugs at the offending fabric with the other, and I help by shifting my buttocks, so he can slide the panties down my thighs.

As he glides them past my ankles, he tsks. "Kailani, these are far more soaked than they should be from the rain." He puts the panties to his nose. "And they smell like your arousal, little warrior. That tells me you've been thinking very naughty thoughts."

He twirls the panties on one strong purple finger and raises one eyebrow. "Tell me what made you get these so extraordinarily wet."

"I…" My face flushes. I'm too timid to tell him about the fantasies spinning in my mind.

"Too shy to talk?" He takes my thighs, one in each powerful hand and spreads them slowly apart. "Wider, Kailani. Yes, like that."

He stands back and admires my body. "You look amazing." His voice is almost reverent. "Look at that gorgeous pussy."

I feel pleased, yet I'm also embarrassed under his scrutiny and start to close my legs.

"No." His voice is sharp. He steps back in and gives me a little slap on one breast—not very hard, but it stings.

"Owh" I gasp in surprise; it doesn't hurt, but the tingle sends a wave of arousal from my belly to my nipples.

"Keep them open until I say otherwise," he commands. "I need to go put this wet garment out to dry. If you move while I'm gone, I'll have to spank you further."

"Yes, Master," I murmur without thinking.

He bends down and kisses the nipple he slapped, then bites it gently.

"Good."

He moves to the back of the cave and arranges the clothing. I force myself to keep my things open as he left them, my whole body aching for his touch. My nipple is wet from his mouth, and I want more, so much more.

I moan and shift—and finally he's back.

His cock is so hard that my eyes must widen because he chuckles.

"Let's see if we can get you to talk," he says conversationally. "Before we move on to other activities."

To my utter surprise, he crouches down and tugs me forward until I'm only halfway seated on the rock, just the back of my buttocks making contact with the stone. He puts my splayed legs over his powerful shoulders and grabs me closer, pulling me to his head.

"You can brace yourself on the rocks behind you," he orders.

"But what…"

I stop talking, and my words turn into a garbled cry as he nestles his head between my legs and licks my clit.

"Stars, Khrys," I manage to get out.

The feeling is like nothing in the world. His tongue is soft like velvet but strong. Dexterous. He swipes along my lower lips, teasing and licking my skin like it's delicious.

"Stars, stars," I chant. My thighs tremble as that incredible feeling of release begins to grow. "I'm going to..."

"No." He pulls his head back. "Not until I give permission. And I won't, not until you tell me about those panties."

"But I can't…" I begin.

He smiles. "I was hoping you'd be difficult."

He stands up and takes me back into his arms and sits on a lower flat rock adjacent to my perch. "A few of these to get you back from the edge," he says.

And then he spanks me. Slap. Slap. Slap. Right across my ass, hard.

"Ow!" I squeal, kicking my legs.

"Quiet," he says and spanks me again. "You'll need to learn to tell me what I need to know, Kailani."

But his voice holds a teasing tone, even under the firm direction, and I know he's enjoying this.

So am I. Each spank presses my core into his rock-hard

thigh and only increases that tingling feeling. I squirm, trying to adjust myself, so I can get the pressure right where I need it.

"You bad little warrior," he says, noticing my actions. He moves me further back, so I can't rub myself against his body and spanks me again.

This time, without the ability to push into his leg, the spanks feel sharper, harder.

"Oooh, ow," I complain, momentarily forgetting about the desire that was growing in my core.

He rubs my skin softly. "Nice and pink. Lovely."

He places me back onto the higher rock and spreads my thighs. "Let's try this again. If you don't tell me what I want, we can do this all day."

He presses his lips to my body and sticks his tongue deep into my cleft. I cry out and grab his horns. They're hard and strong in my hands. I rub them gently, somehow instinctively understanding that it gives him the same feeling I experience.

"Kailani, veck," he mutters, circling his tongue around my clit.

The amazing flutterly circles bring me back to that precipice. I breathe harder and try to push my hips closer to his mouth -

And veck if the bastard doesn't swoop me down over his lap again for more spanks.

"What did I tell you?" He scolds. He's got me adjusted, so I can't grind on him. He spanks my cheeks mercilessly, over and over, as well as the top of my thighs.

Finally I cry out, "This! I wanted this. I was thinking about you. I wanted…"

He stops spanking. "You wanted…?"

"I wanted you to touch me. Bring me pleasure. Like on

the ship. That's what made my panties… wet. I want that amazing feeling."

I'm so embarrassed, I can barely stand it. Thanks stars, I'm over his lap, so I don't need to look into his eyes.

He rubs my bottom again, soothing the place he spanked. "Was that so hard?"

"Yes," I mutter.

"Well, maybe one more lesson to help encourage you to improve your communication," he suggests.

"On your knees, Kailani."

He rubs my ass one more time, then gently places me in front of him. Spreads his thighs, so his gigantic cock juts up, hard and strong.

"Use your mouth, little warrior. Like I did."

"I should…?" I swallow hard and lick my lips. But it doesn't sound unappealing. In fact, I want to take him into my mouth and give him pleasure.

I put my hands on his legs for support and lean in. His cock is so large that I have to open wide to get my mouth around it, but it's not uncomfortable. His skin is soft, and he tastes neutral, with the same clean woodsy scent that I get from his body.

"Suck it and then release and lick," he orders me. "Then suck again. Like that."

I do it, and he takes my head in his hands to guide my motions.

He's firm but not harsh, and as I get into a rhythm, his grip tightens in my hair.

"Veck Kailani, I'm going to come," he mutters.

I suck harder, eager to have this powerful warrior come apart under my ministrations.

With a guttural cry, his cock stiffens, and a spurt of hot

fluid coats my tongue. Startled, I swallow—it's mild and sweet.

I pull back to breathe and, working on instinct, use my hand to continue squeezing his cock as his body tightens, and he spasms in my grip, over and over again.

"It's rainbow!" I exclaim. Even in the dim light from the fire, the swirl of fantastic colors boggles my mind.

He doesn't reply but gives one groan of pleasure and then sighs, a long deep sound of satisfaction.

"Kailani, that was amazing," he murmurs, running his hand through my curls. He cups my shoulder with his palm, his eyes shut.

Seeing him like this, exposed and open to me, makes my heart melt.

Before I can respond, he opens his eyes and smiles. "Now that you finished your lesson, it's time for a reward."

He's all action, once again. "Back on your rock, little one," he orders, putting me back onto the high stone. "Legs nice and wide for my tongue."

I obey eagerly. This time when he puts his lips to my body, it's even more delightful. His movements drive me insane within minutes, and soon I'm squirming.

"Khrys, please, may I come?" I beg.

He chuckles into my body. "Not yet. One more moment."

"But I can't wait!" I'm getting desperate.

"Try hard," he suggests. "Or else I'll have to spank you again. It's just part of learning to obey."

I don't want another spanking—I want the pleasure. So I focus on holding it off.

Finally, the sensation is too strong. "Khrys!" I wail.

"Come, little warrior," he commands, and I do. My whole body contorts as the explosions start and keep coming, over and over.

I hum and squeal and push myself into his obliging mouth to draw out every last drop of pleasure, and when the peak is over, I collapse forward.

He grabs me and cradles me in his arms.

"Look at you, all decorated with my cum," he murmurs, sitting by the fire and putting the blanket back over us. "Stars, how I like the look of you."

I'm so out of my mind with residual pleasure that I don't even really listen. I just lie in his arms, limp and completely satisfied, listening to the rain and the crackling of the fire, feeling his warm arms around me.

This is the best and safest I've felt in... forever.

ailani

Later on, once I've cleaned up and we've donned our newly dried clothes, we sit together again, watching the rain and waiting. Although I still feel a powerful connection with Khrys, looking out at the alien landscape has my anxiety growing as I think about our situation and my future.

"The Kraa never talked about these storms." I stare at the mayhem just feet in front of our faces. "Although they didn't exactly chat with me about all of their adventures."

Now that we're safe—at least for the moment—my mind goes back to the sacks we discarded during our escape. "Do you think the flowers we gathered will survive the storm?"

Khrys is silent for a second. "The bags are strong and waterproof. But we need to go to the craft immediately, Kailani, when we can leave this cave and get to Zandia. We have limited time."

I tense. "No. I need them," I whisper, my whole body numb with disappointment. "I don't understand why we can't take one more solar cycle. Just one. What's the huge rush?"

"We can come back with reinforcements later." He doesn't explain our tight timeframe to me.

"But later means in a few lunar cycles, Khrys." My voice is taut with worry. "Their rainy season is upon us. If we don't get flowers now…" I try not to think about suffering from headaches constantly.

I take a flower from my jacket and eat some of the pollen before stowing the bloom back in the fabric. "These few won't last long." I'm glad I took at least several to keep personally.

He sighs and mutters, "*Veck.* Another spectacular failure."

"What?" I frown, twisting to look up at him.

"Nothing." He shakes his head.

"It sounded like you said, *another spectacular failure.* Remember my ears?" I gesture to my head.

He gives a bitter chuckle. "It's worlds apart from anything that concerns you. You don't care about these things."

I bite my lip. The words come before I can process what they mean: "But I do care. Please tell me."

KHRYS

Zandians don't talk about things like emotions. But for some reason, I find myself opening up to Kailani.

I stare out into the sheets of rain as she breathes quietly in my arms, her body compact between my thighs. "Honor is everything to us on Zandia. Our pride in our work moves our planet forward, makes us successful, decides whether our planet lives or dies. Literally. We've been at war. In my lifetime, we lost our planet and then took it back again."

"Yes?" Her small hand opens on my arm.

I nod. "I've made some mistakes recently. I displeased my

king. Dishonored myself." My voice is full of disgust. "Nothing that can't be fixed, but commanders of my rank— we just don't make mistakes. It's a disgrace."

She's quiet. Then she simply asks, "Why?"

I blink a few times. "Well, I don't know." It's actually not something I've ever considered. "Why? That's…" I shake my head. "Interesting."

"I think the reason a being fails is just as important as the failure itself." Her voice is contemplative. "At least, in my experience."

"Your experience?" I don't mean to sound condescending, but I hear the question in my voice.

"You mean what can a slave know about choices?" Her hair is wet on my shoulder. "Even chattel have secret lives of our own. Decisions to make."

"I'm sorry. I'm sure you do."

"So think about what happened, what led to the failures. Trace it back, and that might give you answers on how to go forward."

Veck, how can she be so wise?

But I frown because images rush back: My unit in battle a few solar cycles ago. The explosive device detonating. The death of my younger brother, the being who mattered most to me in the entire galaxy. The assurances—later, and unconvincing—that it wasn't my fault. That I was an excellent warrior and that deaths happen in battle and that I needed to keep going. To keep training warriors.

It comes to me in dreams regularly, the face of my brother and the other warriors, the look in their eyes as they realize their fate. I usually awake with a guttural cry dying in my mouth, just like they died on that field.

"Khrys?" Her voice is soft, concerned.

"What?"

"Your whole body is locked up."

I realize that I'm grabbing her tightly, my breathing somewhat labored. I relax my muscles. "I apologize." I clear my throat. "Just a memory."

"Must be a bad one." Her voice is even.

"It was." I wipe my brow.

"Do you want to talk about it?"

"Why would I?"

"We humans find that talking can alleviate some of the misery."

"Please don't blame me for being skeptical." My voice is haughty. "Since humans are not currently the reigning masters of the universe."

I wince at my own words, but she doesn't seem fazed. "Exactly. We need strategies to survive our current fate. Talking to each other is one of the best."

"Words solve nothing." I'm clenched up again.

"Won't hurt you to try." She's patient.

The urge for comfort—strangely new—overpowers me. The words tumble out. "This was several solar cycles ago. I was a commander in the army, newly promoted. I trained a troop of Zandians in battle and led them when we took back our planet. But we—failed."

The feeling rises up again, the panic and helplessness. "My brother was one of them."

"I'm so sorry." Her hand is impossibly soft on my arm.

"I think if I had only trained them harder. Pushed faster. Did more. Maybe my brother would've been ready for the attack. Survived."

"Is that what your superiors said?"

I shake my head. "It's what I say to myself. Sometimes the battle plays in my head, over and over. Like a holo that won't stop." I push my temples.

"It sounds tragic. And distracting."

"Perhaps." I consider it. "You know how your body had that instantaneous reaction to the sight of the needle?"

She nods, her blue eyes on the side of my face.

"It's almost like that. Triggers remind me of the battle. I…" I swallow. "I'm a trainer. All of the warriors I train put their lives in my hands—same as my brother. Every mistake I make puts their lives at risk."

"But you make mistakes?"

I nod. "I freeze up—like you did with the needle. Instead of giving the orders I should be giving, I'm suddenly back at the battle, watching my brother die over and over again. And that's when accidents happen."

"I'm sorry," she murmurs.

"That's what happened a few planet rotations ago when I —made my most recent error. I was actually demoted." I give her a side-glance, waiting for scorn or disgust, but it never comes from her; instead, it wells up in my gut. "And it was the right thing for the king to do. I failed at my task."

"You're a great captain, Khrys." Her voice is soft. "I've seen that first hand. You're a clever adversary and a strong warrior. I have no doubt you serve your king well."

"You've not known me enough to make those state-ments." But I feel unaccustomed pride at her compliments.

"It sounds like the ruminations take you away from your tasks. Can you stop thinking of that event quite so often?"

"I deserve to think about him every day and suffer for what happened."

She squeezes my hand. "We humans, the ones the Kraa worked on, we had a technique. We said we'd reserved a certain period of time each solar rotation for worrying about things we can't change. The rest of the time we'd try to focus on living as well as we could despite our circumstances."

"Did that work?" I frown. She said *we*, and I want to follow up on that later, but for now all I can think about is my brother and the memories.

"Not for everything. But even a little bit helps." She strokes my arm.

"And that applies to me how?" My voice is still stiff.

"Do you really think you are honoring his memory by continuing to suffer and doing subpar work? Would he wish this for you or your planet?" She pauses. "Maybe you don't need to punish yourself constantly, especially if it puts others at risk. Think of him each rotation once, and the rest of the time, allow yourself to put the memories aside. At least the part where you castigate yourself."

The idea is like a bolt of lightning. Never once have I considered allowing myself not to suffer at these memories. The concept that I could put down the pain of my brother and move forward is so novel and exhilarating that I blink.

"Perhaps," is all I say to her, though.

She sighs.

"You mentioned...other humans?" I'm eager to change the topic, and I do want to learn about her life and experiences.

"Oh, they made more than one of me. They wanted an army." Now she's the one stiffening up. "Many of their so-called prototypes failed and were eliminated." She looks up at me. "That means killed." Her voice is heavy with anger and pain.

"I assumed as much." My voice is somber.

"They'd bunk several of us together and have us train together." Her voice is contemplative. "Sometimes we'd compete to see who was best at tasks. They didn't want us to join forces, but they learned that humans die faster if they're too isolated." She laughs, a sound with no humor. "Their allowances for us were based solely on monetary value and survival."

"Where are the others?" I stroke her arm.

She swallows and turns her head. "I don't know. They were all sold before I was." Her voice cracks, and she wipes her eyes. "Now it's just me." Whatever happened to the other humans, she's clearly in pain.

"Kailani." I hold her closer. "I'm sorry."

"But I'm away from the Kraa." She sounds surprised, still, at this new twist of fate. "And alive. I'm grateful."

Outside the cave, the hail is gone, and the rain has lessened to a drizzle. The newly formed river below us still roils like it's alive, a thick, silver-gray serpent angrily twisting along the landscape. An entire uprooted tree bobs along like a branch in the furious waters.

"That river is impassable. But at least the sky is calm enough that we could leave the cave." She leans forward and looks up at the gray sky. The two suns are hidden behind thick clouds, but a single wan ray tentatively shoots out.

"And that's a problem. Because if we can venture out, so can the locals. And you can be sure they're coming for us."

ailani

I CRAWL out of the cave and peer left and right; there are no signs of life at all—no antlex, no natives. Just the roaring water, and beyond it, the fields. And somewhere far in the distance, I assume, our bags of flowers. The sky is still gray, but little patches of silver and pink peek through, making that solitary beam of sun seem friendly. Like nature is on our side.

"We need to get across that water first." Khrys stands beside me, tall and powerful. "We'll find the narrowest part of the wash and lay something across it. Perhaps I can find a tree trunk as a bridge."

But even as he speaks, the water slows down. "Or not. It is seeping into the ground that quickly?" He sounds surprised. "The soil here is different from Zandia."

"That's good for us." I stretch out my calves as the water recedes, almost as quickly as it came. "Khrys, please, can we go back and check for the flowers?"

The supplication in my voice is painful to hear, but without them, I don't know how I'll make it. He looks into my eyes for a long second, clearly trying to make some kind of decision. All I can do is hope he'll choose the path that leads to less pain for me.

He sighs. "All right. But any signs of trouble, and we turn back instantly. Clear?"

I nod immediately. "Yes, Master."

Where did that come from?

He seems as surprised as I, but a slow smile spreads across his face. "I like the sound of that on your pretty lips," he murmurs, leaning in closer.

For a split second, I think he's going to kiss me—and I lean in, dying for the contact, but the sound of a cracking branch has us both whirling.

"Just a falling rock." Khrys points as some boulders loosened by the storm rattle down the hillside into a swatch of broken branches.

His shoulders straighten, and he looks focused. "Let's go."

To my utter joy, we find the tan bags untouched, right where we dropped them. There are no antlex around now, and the unpicked flowers are shredded to a pulp. The once-full field is now a vast marshy wasteland of broken stems and crushed petals, and all of the pollen has been washed away.

"Thank stars these are here." I grab the two sacks I filled as Khrys takes his own. The waterproofing seems to have held, and that makes me almost gleeful with relief.

There's a strange squeak beneath my boot. I scream and jump. "What is it?"

I step backward, ready to attack, heart racing, but it's only a small creature. About the length of my forearm, it's got blueish fur and large golden eyes. It stares up at me from the muck and moves its littles paws upward as if begging for food. *Squeak.*

"Khrys? What is this?" I'm entranced and on guard at the same time. "It's so… cute."

He bends down. "I'll be sword-sliced. It's a whimmit." he laughs. "Master Seke's information didn't say those lived here."

"Is it toxic?" I ask although from his demeanor, I can guess that it's not.

"Not to Zandians or humans. They're a kind of rodent. Not the smartest. Look." He reaches down and touches the thing on its back. "They have no sense of danger."

It immediately arches upward into his hand and makes a loud rumbling noise. "Stupid. I could kill it or eat it at once."

He taps it a little harder. It growls at him as if irritated and stops rumbling.

"But you barely eat." I reach down, too. It sniffs my hand then pushes its nose into my fingers. It rumbles again, louder, but it seems to be a happy sound. "It's adorable." The creature pushes closer and puts its paws on my leg.

Khrys sounds disgusted. "They're a nuisance when we're on missions. I can't stand them. Always getting in the way." He bends down to the whippet. "Shoo! Get out of here." He gives it a little push.

The creature ignores him. It continues to paw my leg.

"You don't have them on your planet?"

He shakes his head. "Thank *veck*, no."

A strange thought occurs to me. "Can we keep it?" I feel a sudden surge of affection for this little beast, who—out of nowhere, and for no special reason—is being, in its own way, kind.

"No." His voice is short and holds no room for debate.

"Absolutely not. The craft isn't fitted for wildlife. And we don't need this—*thing*—back on Zandia."

I shriek out a giggle as it licks my hand with a bright purple tongue. "It likes me."

"It would like a bundle of rocks." Khrys shakes his head. "Come, Kailani. We need to focus." He points. "The craft is back that way. Let's go."

"Okay, I'm—"

A sick sense of deja vu fills me as the zing of an arrow fills my ears.

"*Veck*, the locals are back!" Khrys curses. "They waited for us to find the bags. It's an ambush."

"They're approaching from the north." I assess the area, senses on high alert. My muscles tense in preparation for a fight. I listen and learn the sounds of their feet. My vision clears, and I focus. "At their pace, we have thirty seconds. They've not surrounded us yet. We can run for it before they get close enough to aim properly."

"You can't make it to the craft fast enough." His voice is tense. "It's past your endurance distance. I'll hold them off while you get a head start, then I'll catch up."

"We should fight together." The idea of running on my own fills me with panic.

"No." He snaps it. "On my command, you take your sacks and run to the craft."

He slides a device from his tunic and presses it into my hand without looking, then hands me my laser gun from earlier. "Keep these safe."

He uses his long-range laser gun to knock out the first approaching local, but dozens more appear over the tree line. "The craft is programmed to recognize my biomarkers and open for me. This is an override you can use to get aboard. I preprogrammed it with your fingerprint earlier, just in case. Get yourself there and wait for me."

"But…"

"Go. Now."

He shouts so fiercely that I take off racing, the bags bouncing on my leg, heavy and awkward.

He's right—I can't run as fast or long as he, especially not with a load. This is the only way we can both make it. But I'm terrified.

I hear him roar a battle cry, but I don't look back. Soon I'm far enough away that the screams of the natives are muted, and after a while, I hear nothing but odd squeaks from my bag.

And then I'm at the craft.

∾

Kailani

I know I'm in the right place even though I see nothing because the device in my jacket pocket beeps urgently. When I pull it out and touch the smooth indent with my index finger, it glows green. Symbols I don't understand appear, but I raise the device and point it in front of me.

Like magic, the craft shimmers, just at the edges, showing me the outlines of the curved hull and sleek base. The staircase hovers as if half formed

I lurch forward and climb, and the door slides open with a pneumatic hiss. I toss myself inside, and when the door closes behind me, I sob with relief.

I'm alive, I'm safe, and I have the flowers. The *vecking* *f*lowers. I use the curse Khrys says, liking the way it sounds. It's a powerful word.

"*Veck*," I mutter. I'm shaking. I drop into a seat on the craft, allowing myself to catch my breath then get up.

I suck down a nutrition tube and wrap myself in the silver blanket to warm up, standing at the port hole to peer out. Where is Khrys? He's nowhere in sight. To my horror, the sky darkens.

"Where is he?" I mutter.

Squeak.

"What the stars?" I jump back. A lump unfurls itself from the top of the first flower sack. Sodden and dismal, but seemingly unharmed, it's the whimmet from the field.

Squeak. It looks at me with its huge eyes.

"How did you get here?" I blink at the animal. "Were you hiding in my sack?"

Squee. It comes closer and winds around my legs, in and out. It has a pathetic-looking tail of snarled and matted fur, full of burrs and grass. It shakes itself and drops of muddy water fly around my boots.

"You don't belong here." But I can't resist bending down and touching the top of its head. It's ridiculously soft. "You're supposedly a vermin." But its nonjudgmental affection warms my heart, and I stroke it again.

It juts its chin into my thumb, as if enjoying the feeling of my fingers. *Squee.*

"I don't have time for this!" I stand and pace to the port again. No Khrys.

On a whim, I sit down at his flight console and point the small hand device at the screen.

A musical chime rings out and the screen lights up with symbols and numbers.

I remember seeing him tap and glide his fingers along it and in front of the air earlier. There's a symbol of an ear, so I touch it, and the screen cycles through languages. A few I don't know, and then—Ocretion, the most common language in the galaxy.

"Start engines, Captain?" queries the screen. My pulse quickens.

I could leave. Right now. I have my flowers. I have a ship. I could be free—a free human in a galaxy in which we're all enslaved. I don't know where I'd go, but I could figure it out. I could try to find Jesel.

I hesitate. I look outside, where a few drops of rain are starting to flick the ports.

I have no business doing anything except waiting for Khrys. But the idea of escaping grows stronger. My heart races.

"Yes. Start engines. Prepare for takeoff."

"Affirmative."

Lights flash and beeps ring out as the ship begins—apparently—to ready itself for imminent departure. Engines deep within the structure hum to life and a barely discernible thrum, like a heartbeat, comes up through my boots and into my body.

"Starter engines ignited."

It feels good. It feels like safety—and freedom. Things I've never known. Things I've wanted as long as I've been alive.

"Booster engines ready. Thrusters ready. Hyperdrive ready. Preparing life systems."

There's just one thing flashing red, waiting to enable.

I could leave—without Khrys. I could take off with this craft—this priceless piece of tech that can practically fly itself—and find a free planet. It's not impossible.

"I'm smart," I whisper.

The whimmet leaps to my lap and presses itself to my chest. *Squeak.*

"I could learn," I say, resting one hand on the console. "I could figure it out. And if I crash—oh well. At least I gave it my best shot. At least I wouldn't be a slave any longer."

I think about my friends—Ina and Anya, Agniezka and Ruta. "Are they alive?" I ask.

There's no being who can answer me.

"Are they at an auction too, being sold for stein? Maybe they're still on Reneron." That's the way station where Kraa like to store their auctionable items before heading over to the sales planet. "Instead of going to Zandia, I could find them. Save them."

I find that I seem to be speaking to the whimmet, who looks up at me with her golden eyes (I think it's a she) like she's listening.

Rrrrr, she agrees, whipping her furry blue tail along my arm.

I wince. "Stop that. You're full of mud," I chastise her, but my voice is gentle.

"I miss them," I whisper to the whimmet, my eyes blurring with tears. She settles into my lap and pushes her paws rhythmically into my leg.

"Life systems enabled. Craft is ready for liftoff." The ship's console flashes with green. "Awaiting command."

I chew my lower lip. The rain beats down on the ship even harder. Soon it will probably be hail.

The fact that Khrys hasn't returned probably means he's dead. That thought brings a crippling stab of pain, right through the center of my chest, but I push it aside. I need to think this through. The longer I wait, the longer I increase the chance of the locals finding and attacking the ship.

But what if Khrys is still out there—alive? What if he needs my help? My heart twists in my chest and anguish makes me stand.

STOLEN BY THE ZANDIAN

The whimmit leaps to the ground gracefully. *Rrrrr*, she says.

"What if he needs me?"

I look to the console. All I need to do is push one button, and I'll be free, on my own.

But then I see Krhys' face in my mind. Feel his touch. Remember the closeness we felt in the cave.

The console repeats. "Awaiting command."

Sweet Mother Earth. What should I do?

CHAPTER 9

*K**hrys***
 The shooting goes on far longer than I expect.

Arrows fly towards me in carefully-planned volleys—these locals are smart. Part of me admires their tenacity and ability to craft such weapons with rudimentary tech. The other part of me just wants to survive.

"Get back, *veck* you," I mutter. My weapon is set to high stun; I don't want to kill. But if they don't back off soon, I'll be forced to do what's necessary. "You idiots. Don't make me kill you."

At first, I just held them off long enough to give Kailani a head start. I planned to run as soon as I was sure she'd made it to the ship. But when I ran, fresh groups appeared on all sides and cornered me against an outcropping of rocks. They approach through the sodden flower field, slowly but surely. The dozen or so of them in the lead have now lifted up what look to be rough animal hide shields that are protecting the archers behind them.

But their heads are still visible. To my relief, my good

eye and fast weapon drop over half of the visible archers, and the arrows slow. The group raises shields and gathers in a circle.

Stars, their maneuvers are surprisingly modern. I adjust my laser gun to the burn feature and launch a series of fast laser strikes at the shields. When the hides burst into flames, I whisper, "Yes!"

Screams of horror and dismay rise up from the group, who finally turn and race away from me, apparently having decided it's not worth it—right now.

"Finally," I mutter. I look once more to ensure they're really going, and then run for my craft. I'm concerned about Kailani.

Vecking stars, if she encountered more locals on the way back, I would not be able to live with myself. What if she had another panic attack?

Excrement. I run as fast as I can, but in the distance, I see the ship unmask, the engines running at full launch power.

Veck.

She's *vecking* leaving me. The ship is departing.

Kailani has betrayed me—she's about to flee with my craft, leaving me here alone on this planet.

"That cursed human," I sputter, as the sky booms and rain pours out like a waterfall. I'm blinded by the sheet of water, but suddenly an apparition wavers through the streams of liquid. I raise my laser gun at a misshapen figure tromping toward me, but something makes me hold my fire. The figure swims into focus as it approaches.

"Khrys? Khrys!"

My heart stutters. Stars! It's Kailani, wearing a set of far-too-big Zandian gear, tramping doggedly through the storm.

She waited.

She didn't leave without me. She could have—stars, she

probably thought about it. But she didn't. She came out to find me.

Hail starts to tear through her garment. "Kailani!" My voice is instantly lost in the storm. She doesn't hear me. I run toward her.

She holds up her laser gun, pointed at me.

"Kailani, it's me." I grab the weapon from her hands before she can shoot. "It's Khrys."

"Khrys! Thank the sweet Mother Earth!" She throws her arms around me in a stranglehold.

She waited. My heart can't stop celebrating. My human had everything she needed to escape—the ship, her medicine, a weapon. But she didn't leave.

She has truly bonded to me. *Veck*, is it what the humans call love? This means...she's mine. She claimed me. I'm going to claim her right back.

"Come on, let's go!" I tug her aboard the craft as the hail starts to pound the ground with vehemence, the spiked balls even bigger than before.

We collapse onto the floor in a wet heap, panting.

"Awaiting command," says the console.

I scramble into action. I sit at the station and program the route to Zandia, avoiding the asteroid belts and the danger zones where we know Ocretion ships lurk lately. Then I launch us into space.

Kailani

THE MOMENT KHRYS launches us into space and we're safely away, he gets up from the console and stalks toward me. I'd buckled in for the takeoff, but now I unbuckle, trying to discern whether he's angry or…

He reaches for me, grasping me behind the head and yanking my mouth to his. "Kailani," he growls after a searing kiss.

I blink up at him, stunned by his intensity.

He doesn't stop to explain. He captures my mouth again, sweeping his tongue between my lips at the same time he picks me up to straddle his waist. "I'm going to *veck* you so hard," he growls.

"Oh." The startled syllable tumbles from my lips. Thrills of excitement zing through my nether regions. I reach up to squeeze one of his horns, and he groans, shooting forward. He carries me to the washroom, where he lowers me to my feet, his lips still twisting over mine. He strips my wet clothes from my body.

I slide my hands under his tunic, my palms exploring the ridges of his abdominals. As soon as he has me naked, he pushes me into the washtube. Even though it's tiny, I tug him in after me. "I-I think we can both fit." I'm breathless.

He kicks off his boots and leggings and follows me in, pressing my back and ass against the wall when his enormous body fills the tube. He hits the button, and the door closes.

I reach up on my tiptoes and grasp both his horns.

"*Veck*, Kailani," he groans, palming my ass. His huge erection presses against my belly.

I squeeze and pump his horns marveling at how his cock seems to respond as if I'm squeezing him there. He thrusts against me, his kisses growing even more brutal.

"Take me," I plead, just before the water covers us both. It doesn't stop Khrys from kissing me. He hoists me up, lifting my hips to match the height of his, and the moment the water drains from our faces, he thrusts in.

I gasp, and he goes still, buried inside me. He leans his forehead against mine. "Okay, little warrior?"

I nod. "Yes, Master." The title feels right. If I am to have a master, he's the perfect one for me. So thoughtful and caring. Protective and kind. Dominant in the perfect ways.

He eases back and thrusts in again.

My eyes roll back with the pleasure of it. He's in so deep. So far. He owns my body in a way the Kraa never did. In a way that my body revels in.

"Yes," I encourage, squeezing his horn.

He thrusts again, deep and hard. And again.

"More," I murmur.

He picks up speed. His movements are powerful. Almost frightening, but the pleasure by far outweighs any fear I might have that he could hurt me.

Besides, I know if I didn't like it, he'd stop. I believe that now. I can trust him.

"Kailani," he groans. The sound of my name in those guttural tones makes me just as wild for him as he is for me. I squeeze my legs around his back and use my heels to drive him in harder with each thrust, faster.

The air blowers stop, and the door slides open, but we're not going anywhere. Khrys pounds into me, his powerful body melding with mine, mastering me, devouring me.

"*Veck*, I can't hold back," he mutters.

"Don't," I pant. "Don't hold back."

He shouts out a roar and buries himself deep inside me. The heat of his cum fills me as I crest the peak as well, my inner walls squeezing and milking his cock for all his seed.

"Khrys," I cry out brokenly.

"Kailani. Sweet human. My beautiful, wonderful human."

❧

K<small>HRYS</small>

I <small>CARRY</small> Kailani to the bunk room and drop her on the bed. "Have you had your medicine?"

She nods, her blue gaze locked on mine, pupils wide. Her face flushes a lovely shade of golden-pink. She looks well-*vecked*.

Content, even.

I *vecking* love that look on her, and I vow to put it on her face every *vecking* planet rotation.

If I can keep her, that is.

I'll have to petition King Zander for permission to mate her. He may refuse me. She's very valuable. He may wish her to be mated to more than one Zandian male because her genes may be particularly useful for the future generations.

That thought makes me want to punch the ship wall.

The king may not even grant me a mate after what I've done. Although if Kailani's body provides the answers to heal Princess Kaylar and the other sick halflings, I feel certain he'll be grateful.

"Did you eat something? Are you hungry?"

She shakes her head. "No, Master."

Veck. Every time she calls me that, I want to roar my satisfaction to the stars. Nothing has ever sounded more perfect to my ears.

"Good, because now I'm going to claim you again." I crawl over her and cage her wrists gently, then press them down beside her head. "Tell me something, little warrior. You thought about leaving without me back there, didn't you?"

Her pupils shrink, and her breath catches. I lean down and do what I've been dying to do since the moment I first saw her at the auction—take one of her perky brown nipples into my mouth. I swirl my tongue around it then nip it with my teeth.

"Hmm? You figured out how to start the ship. One command, and you could've left me behind."

"But I didn't," she whispers.

I give her a slow, feral smile. "No, you didn't. Do you know why?"

She gives her head a slow roll side to side.

I settle a little of my weight on top of her, my cock long between her legs. I give her neglected nipple the same treatment. She rolls her hips to meet mine.

"Because you know you belong to me now, don't you? I'm going to take care of you. I'm your master."

"I-I was afraid you needed my help," she admits, and my heart squeezes.

"You were worried about me." My smile grows wider.

"Yes."

I crawl lower on her body and push her knees wide. "Here I was thinking a little punishment was in order. But I think, instead, it should be reward." I lick into her.

She jerks as if shocked by the sensation, her knees closing around my shoulders. "Khrys!" she cries out. When she grasps both my horns, I suck in my breath, nearly coming a second time without warning.

"*Veck*, Kailani. I'm not sure you realize what you're doing to me."

She gives me a knowing smile—so full of confidence and power it floors me. "I think I do," she purrs. I slip my tongue between her folds, tracing the dainty lips. "What was my punishment going to be?" she asks, like she's sorry I removed it from the agenda.

I flick my tongue over her pleasure-button, and her knees slap my shoulders again. She lifts her hips off the bed to press her sex against my mouth. I push pin them down and affix my lips over her tiny nubbin, sucking.

"Oh….oh!" Her knees flap around my ears.

"I don't know, a little spanking. Maybe on your pussy this time."

She leans up on her elbows, eyes wide. "H-how?"

I grin. "Like this, beautiful." I push one of her knees up high, toward her shoulder, to open her to me, then bring my fingers down lightly over her clit in a tiny spank.

She jerks, her flat belly shuddering in and out. "Yes," she whispers.

I start to do it again, but a strange sound makes me leap and whirl, ready to attack. "What the—"

The little whimmet from the field has jumped onto the cot behind me. I grab for it, and it bites my hand—not hard; its flat teeth couldn't damage a sheet of silk, but it clearly doesn't care for me.

"*Vecking* nuisance," I curse, wiping my hand along the blanket.

"Don't hurt Whimmie!" Kailani exclaims.

It takes just a moment for me to quiet my reflexes, and then I boom with laughter. "You brought that creature on the ship?"

"She stowed away in the flower bag. Isn't she adorable? She's the one who told me I needed to go out and find you in the storm."

I chuckle. "Is that so?"

"Yes! Can I keep her?"

I pick the purring creature up and set it gently on the floor, away from us. It protests, gracefully leaping back up.

"I don't think she'll be allowed on Zandia, Kai, but I'll see what we can do." I pick the silly would-be pet up again and drop it to the floor. "There are consequences for bringing live animals on my ship without permission, though."

Kailani leans up on her elbows, her beautiful breasts sliding as she moves. "What are they?" Her eyes glitter with interest.

"I'll show you." I move back and lift her toned legs, holding both her ankles in one hand in the direction of the ceiling. I deliver a slap to her exposed ass.

Her cry sounds far more wanton than pained. I deliver a few more spanks. In this position, her sex is exposed between her legs, and I can spank her there as well. "Oh! Ow. Ung." I spank until her ass turns a lovely shade of pink, and then I lower her hips back to the cot. "Roll over, little warrior. Show me that red ass."

Kailani only looks unsure for a moment, and then she obeys, rolling to her belly and looking over her shoulder at me.

"On your knees, precious." I pull her hips up, so she rests on her knees. When she tries to rise to her hands, I press my hand between her shoulder blades to keep her torso down. "Just like that." I rub my cock over her dripping entrance. "Good girl," I murmur when she relaxes, and I ease in.

"Mmm," she hums, apparently enjoying the sensation of being filled by me again.

"You take my cock like such a good girl," I praise. I grip her hips and give her a few short bumps, slapping her ass with my loins on each in-stroke.

She moans, loud and long.

The silly whimmit tries to jump up on the bed again, and Kailani giggles, pushing it off.

I go slowly, with several long strokes in and out, glorying in the sensation of my cock cooling each time it leaves her tight channel and then sinking into her delicious heat again. I press my thumb to her anus and massage it. "When you're really naughty, I'll *veck* you here," I tell her, my cock thickening even more at the thought. Her back pucker squeezes and flutters at the threat.

"Khrys," she moans. "Please."

"You need it faster, my little warrior?"

"Yes, Master."

Veck. I start to lose control again. I grip her hips and slam in hard, unable to hold back. I thrust into her with such force that she stretches her arms out to brace herself against the wall. I reach around and rub her swollen clit.

She cries out, her muscles contracting around my cock.

It's all I can take. I shout and pound into her, my balls drawing up tight, my thighs quaking. "Kailani!" Veck. I plow in and out, lights dancing behind my eyes, and then I come with a roar loud enough to fill the entire ship.

My vision goes black for a few moments. When it clears, I find Kailani, gasping and giggling beneath me.

"Sweet little warrior." I ease out and drop beside her, pulling her into my arms. "I should have known you'd steal my heart."

ailani

The trip to Zandia is shorter than I think we both want it to be. I'm nervous about what it will be like to live on Zandia with Khrys. He hasn't specifically said he will mate me, but considering how many times he's pleasured me in the past planet rotation, it seems obvious that I'm his.

Khrys seems to grow tense as we approach. When he opens the comms to announce our landing, his voice is deep and terse.

"Is everything all right?" I ask, prickles of warning starting to crawl up my arms.

He lands the craft expertly—a whisper soft touch to the ground then swivels in the flight chair and looks at me. His brown eyes are troubled. "Kailani, there's something I should tell you."

The prickles race everywhere. "What is it?" My stomach tightens.

"The reason I went to get you from the auction is... "

I leap to my feet, terror streaking through me.

"Remember I told you about the epidemic?"

"What?" My mind spins, trying to figure out what Khrys is trying to tell me.

The conversation is cut off by the whoosh of the door seals, and I blink at the new bright lights streaming in from the tarmac. A flurry of voices and activity assaults my senses. A handful of Zandians flood the craft.

I scoop up Whimmie when she gives a cry of alarm.

"Captain Khrys, you must come with us," one of the guards announces.

"Why do they have weapons?" I'm taken aback by the sight of alert warriors flanking me and Khrys. "I don't understand." I turn to Khrys, that terrible feeling burgeoning in my stomach.

"Kailani, I took this ship without leave, and I'll have to answer for it, but it's going to be all right." He speaks quickly as the guards on either side of him take his arms. He shakes off their hold. "I'm coming peaceably, there's no need for restraint," he snaps.

I squeeze Whimmie tightly, and she squeaks in alarm.

"Khrys?" My voice is high and panicked. With a tremble. "What is this? What's going on?"

"Welcome to Zandia." One of the Zandians—he appears to be a commander—looks me up and down, and his voice—although not angry—doesn't sound warm and inviting. "Captain Khrys, you will accompany Gabin for questioning. Kailani, please come with us to the isolation med chamber." It's not a request.

Isolation med chamber.

The words strike fresh terror through my body.

"Give her a moment," Khrys barks as the warriors beside him attempt to pull him off the craft. They move him down the ramp, and he calls out over his shoulder, "She's been traumatized by her former masters. You have to go slowly. She's afraid of needles!"

What in the name of Mother Earth is going on? Did Khrys just sell me out? He stole me from auction only to turn me over for more medical experiments? I'm such an idiot! I knew he couldn't be trusted!

I double over as if to heave, but nothing comes out.

"Come, Kailani," the commander says.

"I'm not going anywhere with you," I snap at the male who addressed me, heart hammering. I carefully place Whimmie on a seat and prepare to fight. I glance around for my med kit—it's across the bay, too far to reach. "Let. Khrys. Go."

"Khrys must answer for his actions, but I expect he will be released. Especially if our medical team finds you to be as useful as we hope."

We hope?

Medical team?

"No." I crouch in a fighting stance. "No medical team is touching me. I didn't agree to this."

The commander's brows dip, but he doesn't look angry. More confused. "No harm will come to you, Kailani. Did Khrys not speak to you about this? We have a critical need for your cells to fight the Z4-A virus that's infected our young human population."

The epidemic. That's what Khrys was trying to tell me.

But the asshole never said anything about using me—using my cells—to cure it. How could he? Did he actually use me as a pawn to buy his own freedom for his mistakes on Zandia?

Pain rips through my heart, equal to the anger.

I leap in an attack, kicking the commander and nearly capturing the sword at his waist. In a flash and flurry of movement, the powerful Zandian warriors have me subdued, howling with rage.

"Take her to the med bay," the commander says. "Bayla can calm her down there."

"I won't go anywhere!" I scream, writhing and twisting in their grasp, but I can't get free. They drag me off the ship. "Let me go!"

"Dr. Daneth," I hear the commander speak in clipped tones. "The patient is uncooperative. We're going to need a sedative, so she doesn't hurt herself."

In the distance, I see Khrys turn from where he's being escorted away. "Kailani!" He sounds alarmed. "Let her go!" He breaks free and sprints toward us, but moments later, he's tackled to the ground.

"*Veck* you, Khrys," I scream at him, using his curse word. "You sold me out! I hate you! I will never forgive you for this!"

When he's hauled to his feet, he doesn't make another attempt to break free, but he won't let them drag him away, either. He stands, watching me kick and fight, anguish marring his usual impassive face.

"No med bay, no med bay," I chant as they propel me forward. No one has hurt me, but I can't seem to free myself from their restraint.

"They have to ensure you're healthy," one of them says.

"And isolate you for your own protection prior to your donation," says another. "The doctor needs to keep you in a sterile environment before any surgical procedures."

"The medical team is eager to extract your cells. Your gift may be the answer they've been looking for."

Tears prick my eyes. No more experiments. No more surgeries.

Somehow it all seems so much worse now that I had a

taste of freedom. I believed it was over. That I'd see waterfalls and be in charge of my own medicine.

But I'm not going to be free. I'm right back in captivity, a breathing lump of flesh owned by others, subject to their whims and desires.

I make another attempt at freedom, fighting the two Zandians holding me until I end up on the ground with one sitting on top of me.

"Get off her, or I'll cut your vecking head off," a furious Khrys roars. He holds a sword to the throat of the Zandian on top of me. Gabin, the warrior who'd held him before, stands at his back, as if willing to allow his intervention.

The guard slowly eases back. "I'm just following orders, Captain. I tried not to hurt her."

"I'm not hurt," I bite out, fury making it impossible to feel anything else.

"Talk to her," Gabin advises. "See if you can calm her down."

"Kailani—I'm sorry. I should have discussed it before we landed. We have young here who are sick. Your body holds the key to helping them survive." His voice is full of supplication. "We just need some blood and bone marrow tissue—"

I slap his face as hard as I can.

He betrayed me. He fucking betrayed me.

My breath comes faster and in odd short bursts. Black and yellow static swirl in front of my eyes

"They won't hurt you. They just need some samples. After that—"

"No," I whisper, backing up. "No samples. I can't. You know I can't!" I crouch down and vomit.

"Take her now," the commander says. "She needs help."

"Let me take her," Khrys entreats, but the warrior Gabin takes his arm. "You're only making it worse," he says.

The two warriors take me by the arms. "You'll be okay very soon," one of them promises me. "We're taking you to Doctor Daneth."

He says this like it's supposed to bring comfort. Instead, I nearly swoon from the panic. The hyperventilation starts. The taste of the vomit is acrid in my mouth.

One of the warriors walks by holding Whimmie with his thumb and middle finger away from his body like she's diseased.

I scream. "Don't hurt her!" I wail. "She's mine! She's mine. Please." I collapse completely, my feet dragging like a limp doll.

A Zandian picks me up with ease although his arms are dispassionate. "Hurry," he says to his companion. "She's precious to Zandia. We need to get her to the doctor immediately."

The last thing I remember before blacking out is the sound of my hiccupped breaths and the pain of a headache breaking my skull apart in a million pieces.

hrys

I've never experienced pain like this before—not even when my brother died. It's all true what they say about human females. They activate emotions in us. Bring us to life. Make us vulnerable to this life-crushing heartache.

Because Kailani—the beautiful, strong, sweet being I vowed to protect—feels betrayed by me.

Veck!

I did betray her. It was my own idiocy in not explaining the situation. I put it off, wanting to win her trust, to bond her to me. But I should have told her before we landed. Instead, I selfishly claimed her again and again, forgetting about what was important.

Zandia.

Except that doesn't feel right.

Not Zandia—*Kailani.*

Stars, yes. It's true. That female means more to me than my honor. Even more than aiding the ailing halflings. If I'd handled myself better, it wouldn't be a choice. If I'd been able to convince Kailani to help before we arrived.

Veck it all! This is my worst mistake of all.

Gabin leads me into an interrogation room and sits with me. "You're to wait for the council, I believe."

When I don't answer, he says, I'm sorry, my friend."

I shake my head. "No, I deserve this and more. All of it. My mate—"

Gabin's eyebrows shoot up. "Did you mate her? Without permission? I didn't see any piercings."

I drop my head into my hands. "No, not officially. But I claimed her, Gabin. She trusted me. And right now, she's afraid and alone, and I'm here in this holding cell for questioning, unable to do anything."

Gabin shakes his head. "It didn't seem to me like she wanted you there."

The terrible weight on my chest grows even heavier. "*Veck*. I know. I never told her why we wanted her. She's been traumatized by her former masters. She hates doctors and needles and surgeries. I didn't want to scare her. I thought I'd win her trust first. But I made it so much worse."

"Not worse," Gabin says, but I know he's just being kind.

"I need to be with her. Even if she doesn't want me there. We've bonded."

Gabin's wrist comm lights up. "Take Captain Khrys to a holding cell. The king doesn't want to see him until the human has been evaluated."

I shoot to my feet. "No!" I shout. "That's too late. Master Seke, my mate is highly distressed. At this point, she is unwilling to give any samples. Are we going to force her? Treat her as badly as the rest of the galaxy treats humans?"

Seke's holo spins to look at me. "Captain, her reluctance is precisely why you're going to a holding cell. Your methods of extracting her may not have been honorable. We need full information before any action is taken."

I curse and fall back to my chair.

And then a terrible realization hits me.

"She needs her medication," I snap. "The one we went to Dentron to gather flowers for. If she doesn't get it, she suffers horribly."

"Where is the medication?" Master Seke asks coolly.

"On the ship. I must get it now." I'm already running out the door, without leave.

Kailani

I WAKE INTO A NIGHTMARE. Two beings hover over me, peering down with great concentration, one a Zandian, the other one apparently a human female.

"Her vitals are strong, and she's free of any infectious agents," the male declares. "But adrenaline levels are high, and her cortisol is dangerously elevated. She'll need to rest and relax before we can begin the testing." He sounds displeased at this. "Those need to come back to normal levels first."

As they come into focus, I realize he holds a syringe.

I scream and jerk.

The human flinches in surprise, but the Zandian doesn't react. His expression is cool. "She's awake," he says to his companion. He sets the syringe down on a shiny tray. "Calm her, please."

My whole body begins to tremble. I lurch up to a sitting position. "No," I struggle. "Get away from me."

The syringe gleams in the light.

The human's voice is gentle and soft. "We're not going to hurt you, Kailani. We're going to give you something to help you relax."

I'm confused by the fact that it's a human working on me. A human in some position of power over me.

"Where's my whimmet?" I have no idea why I'm asking about the animal now. Maybe because with Khrys' betrayal, that little furry creature is the only being I trust.

"Your what?" The human blinks at me, her eyebrows arched up into a query.

"The animal I found. It was on the craft with me."

"I'm sorry, I don't know anything about that." She hands me a fluid tube. "Please drink this, yes? You need to rehydrate."

I ignore the fluid. "They didn't hurt her, did they?" My stomach is a rock. Pain starts to reverberate in my skull.

The doctor steps forward, the needle prepped in his gloved hand.

"No! Don't touch me." I'm hoarse with panic. They don't seem to have me tied down, but I'm dizzy and nauseated. My headache is coming on swiftly.

I look around me for any ways to escape. I'm in a small room that's mostly white and silver—it looks like a med bay. The door is secure, and the window, if it even opens, doesn't seem easily accessible.

I jump down from the table in a crouch. "I don't want to hurt you, but I will," I warn.

The Zandian instantly steps protectively in front of the dark-haired human. "You will do no such thing," he snaps.

"It's going to be all right." The human sounds so kind. She touches the Zandian's arm in a gesture that appears more intimate than a master-slave or even boss-employee. "It's normal to be disoriented on your first planet rotation here. Many humans have this kind of reaction. But you're on Zandia now. You're safe."

I eye the needle, panic surging again. "Let me out of here. You have to let me out of here. I won't let you experiment on me." A terrible trembling starts through my limbs. I kick the needle out of the Zandian's hand. At least I try to, but he quickly side-steps and wraps an arm around my chest.

"I'll sedate her. She's too agitated to reason with. We'll try again later," he says to his assistant.

"No!" I scream, jabbing him with my elbow and almost managing to get free.

"Stop!" Khrys roars, appearing in the doorway. "Unhand her."

The doctor does release me, but he speaks evenly to Khrys. "You do not give the orders in my lab, Captain."

"She requires medication. Can't you see she's in the throes of pain?"

I realize, then, that he's holding the box with my medication. Despite my fury with him, that fact produces an instant response in my body. Relief. Desperate need. The desire to do anything he tells me to do in order to get the meds.

I rush to him, and he scrambles to open the box, producing the dropper. I part my lips, and he dribbles it into my mouth.

"Come with me," Khrys orders, catching my hand.

"No," the doctor barks. "She's not cleared to leave the—"

"Dr. Daneth, I know what's at stake here. But my mate is frightened and unwilling at this point to assist, and I must insist she be remanded to my care to ensure her emotional well-being."

I blink, the throbbing in my head starting to ebb. My pain-muddled brain stutters on several parts of his statement at once. *My mate. Unwilling at this point to assist. Emotional well-being.*

I pull my hand out of his grasp and slap him hard across the face. He doesn't dodge or parry, he just takes it, regret washing over his expression.

"Captain Khrys, clearly you are responsible for her emotional upset," Dr. Daneth says.

"No, he's not! You are!" I scream at the doctor. For some reason—angry as I am at Khrys —I feel the need to protect him. "You all are." I glare at every being in the room. "But you better not hurt Kyrs. If anyone is going to hurt Khrys, it will be me." I slap Khrys once more for good measure. "LIke this."

The doctor makes a noise that might be irritation. "This is highly irregular and inappropriate." He looks at Bayla then back at me. "You need to settle down, so we can proceed."

"Doctor Daneth." Khrys' voice is firm and convincing. "You're right; she's angry at me, and she has every right. I'd like the chance, anyway, to explain things to her. Help her understand what's at stake." He meets the doctor's gaze. "I don't think she'll be able to settle down until she feels safe and secure. I can help do that for her."

Even though I'm angry beyond belief at Khrys, being near him still has an oddly calming effect. I'm relieved that he's all right. When they took him from me, I was so terrified for him—

I take a deep breath.

The wristband on my arm beeps. One of the red lights has turned yellow. Another one starts to blink green.

"Interesting." The doctor glances at my wrist. "It appears that being around you does seem to help her vitals improve." He frowns.

Bayla steps closer and looks into my eyes. "Do you want to go with Captain Khrys right now, Kailani?"

I nod.

Bayla looks at the doctor. They seem to have a conversation without words. She tilts her head; he nods.

"All right." The doctor crosses his arms. "You may leave the med bay for a short time." He touches my wrist and looks at Khrys. "But if these turn red, you must bring her back for her own safety."

I ignore him and promptly take Khrys' hand back in mine. "Let's go." I'm moving to the door before Khrys. The moment we're out of the lab, I start running. Khrys keeps my hand tight in his, keeping pace.

We're in some kind of marble-floored building—more beautiful and expensive than any I've seen. Nothing like the kinds of medical buildings I've known before.

"This way." Khrys tugs me down a corridor then out a door. We burst outside, and I draw up, blinking in the afternoon light.

"Where are we going?"

"Anywhere you want to go, little warrior," Khrys says softly. "The waterfall. My domicile. Off-planet, somewhere. It's up to you, just know that you won't be going alone. Anywhere you go, I go. You're my mate."

I turn and face him, my eyes filling with tears. "Khrys, what's happening?"

Guilt and regret wash over his face. "Let's go to the waterfall, and I'll tell you everything. I'm sorry, Kailani. I'm so *vecking* sorry. I never meant for things to happen this way."

"What way?" One of my tears spills, hot and hurried, down my face.

He takes my face in his hands, thumbing away the moisture. "Come with me. Please? And I'll tell you everything."

I nod, another tear tracking down my face. Because what other choice do I have? It's Khrys or that horrible med bay back there. Even if I want to kick Khrys in the nuts, I'd take him over a doctor any day.

I'd take him over any being.

"What about Whimmie?" I ask, remembering the only other being who seems to care for me right now.

Khrys pauses in surprise. "We'll get her, too. All right? I may end up in the dungeons for this but..."

"But what?" I tip my face up to his, trying to figure it all out.

"You're what's important to me."

CHAPTER 12

 *hrys*

I TAKE Kailani's hand and lead her to my hovercraft, which I fly to the clearing above the waterfall. I appear to be in luck —there are no other crafts parked in the area. We will have the waterfall to ourselves.

She eyes me nervously. I've lost her trust, and it won't be easy to recover. She still seems to think I'm trying to trick her.

"Come on. You're going to love this," I promise, taking her hand and jogging with her toward the falls. She runs along beside me, picking up speed when she hears the sound of the crashing water.

We circle around where twin waterfalls cascade over zandian crystals, sending rainbow prisms in all directions. Kailani stops and gasps.

"Oh! It's beautiful."

I squeeze her hand, grateful when she doesn't pull out of my grasp.

"The water is warm. One waterfall is hot, one is cold, so the pool below is the perfect temperature." I strip off my clothes.

I know we need to talk, but I'd do anything to show her something nice right now. Something beautiful.

She nibbles her cheek, then strips out of her clothes, too.

"Do you know how to swim?"

She answers me by jumping into the water ahead of me. I smile and follow her in. She's a fantastic swimmer, and she kicks straight toward the waterfalls, diving under them and then reappearing, smiling.

I'm not as skilled. I spent half my life in space, training on King Zander's palatial pod after we lost our planet. We had no opportunities for swimming there, but my body still remembers how to stay afloat and how to propel myself around. I follow Kailani's sleek form under the waterfalls. She swims beneath them and discovers the secret moss-covered ledge behind them.

"So you didn't lie about the waterfall," she says grudgingly, pulling herself out of the water to examine the crystal wall. My horns stiffen at the sight of her fully naked and out of the water, but I shove my lust down.

"I didn't lie about anything. Zandians don't lie." I climb out of the water and sit on a soft patch of moss.

She whirls, hurt and anger marring her lovely face. "What did you omit, then?"

I try to swallow against the tight band around my throat. "A Z4-A virus has affected the planet. Not the Zandians, but the weaker humans. Many of the young—the halflings we're relying on keeping our species alive, including the king's own daughter, Kaylar. Some have died already."

She's gone still and tense. "I see."

"When I saw your dossier, I hoped your engineered resistance to illness might provide some answers. To save the children."

"And you thought you'd be a hero and save your species by bringing me here."

I rub my face. "*Veck*, Kailani. That was my plan, yes. Before I knew you. And then I realized how traumatized you were. How much you hated needles and doctors, and I held back my purpose. I didn't want you to be afraid. But I should have told you everything. And I'm sorry—I'm so *vecking* sorry about the way they took you. I never meant for that to happen. I want to rip all their heads off their *vecking* necks."

She comes over to sit beside me. Some of the tension has left Kailani's face. I doubt I'm forgiven, but maybe she's not as angry as she was before.

"They took me into custody because I hadn't requested permission to go on the mission. I should have accounted for that. I was a fool. I guess I imagined a much more celebratory landing. Me the hero—you the heroine. Instead we were both dragged in like prisoners."

She studies me. "So, what happens now?"

I lift my shoulders. "You don't have to do anything. I won't let them touch you, all right? If you want me to go steal another airship and fly you somewhere else, I will. But I beg you to just give Zandia a chance. Not me—you don't have to ever speak to or see me again if you don't want to. But I didn't lie when I said Zandia was a safe place for humans. You could make friends here. Make a life."

She blinks at me. Her golden skin flushes a bit. "You called me your mate—back in the med bay."

My horns thicken and lean in her direction. I try again to swallow. "I want you as my mate, yes. If you'd have me."

She doesn't answer.

"But matings must be approved by the king. I don't know if I'd be granted the privilege." I pick up one of the tiny crystals on the edge and roll it around between my fingers.

"Especially if I don't help the doctors, right?"

"I'm not certain," I admit.

"Did you just get in more trouble by taking me away from there?"

I shrug. "Possibly. I don't care. You were frightened and alone, and I wasn't going to sit around obeying orders when you were suffering."

"You're an idiot," she says, climbing to her feet.

A stone sinks in my belly. "Yes," I agree.

She loops a leg over me and straddles my lap. "Thank you."

My breath catches. Horns go rock hard. I fill my hands with her ass and yank her hips over my erection as I claim her mouth.

"*Veck*, Kailani."

She rubs her slick pussy over my erection, writhing in my lap. When she reaches down to grip my cock and guide it inside her, I don't hold in my growl of satisfaction. I nip her neck, suck on her nipple. Then I grip her ass and lift and lower her hips over mine. Her glorious breasts bounce in front of my face. She loops her slender arms around my neck and puts her mouth over one of my horns.

I roar with the pleasure of it, yanking her hips in snug against mine, nearly coming. "Stars, Kailani. If you do that again, this will be over way too soon."

Her laugh is husky. "Is that so?" She takes my entire horn into her mouth, her tongue swirling around it. She sucks hard. My thighs quake. Balls draw up tight.

"Kailani," I choke.

She pops off the horn, and I groan, impaling her with my erection as I pull her over me in quick bounces. She swirls that velvety wet tongue around my other horn.

"*Veck, veck, veck,*" I groan. "I won't last another moment."

"Mmm," she hums around my sensitive appendage.

I can't take it any longer. I flip her on her back on the soft moss and slam into her like my life depends on it.

Her head falls back in pleasure. "Yes, Khrys. Yes!"

I've never been happier to hear those words. *Veck*, I thought I'd lost my mate forever back there, and now. she's screaming my name while I pound between her legs. By the one true Zandian star, I don't care if my honor is never restored. This is what matters. This is where I belong.

I force myself to slow down, arcing in and out of her smoothly as I lower my head to tease one of her nipples with my tongue.

She moans and grips my horns, causing me to slam in hard again.

"Little warrior," I murmur. "I need you so vecking much. I love you, Kailani."

She gasps and wraps her legs around my back, pulling me in tight. Her eyes shimmer with tears. "I love you, Master Khrys. My mate."

Her mate.

Veck.

I'm lost.

I brace one hand on the moss and pound into her, leaning my forehead against hers, our panting breaths mingling. For a few moments, time suspends. We are in ecstasy together—the balance point of love and lust and need and everything wonderful. Then, need topples the scales, and I plow into her even harder, making her scream my name until she's hoarse, and we both pitch off the precipice into satisfaction.

Her tight channel squeezes my cock, milking it for its rainbow-hued essence. I kiss her face, her eyelids, her soft, silky hair. "I love you, Kailani," I murmur, knowing without a doubt it's true. Even though love is more of a human expression, not an emotion I ever imagined I'd know.

"I love you."

She lifts her small hand and strokes my face. "I love you, too."

I drop beside her, and we spoon, looking at the waterfall and the myriad of rainbows around the crystal grotto. I search for and find another perfect crystal on the ground and hand it to her.

"Is this the crystal that fuels your bodies?"

"Yes. Zandian crystal. It's used in laser technology and is only found on our planet, so it's what makes us rich. Which is also why our species was nearly wiped out."

"When your planet was invaded."

"Yes, when I was young."

"And your brother died taking it back."

"Yes."

The sound of voices cuts through the roaring of the water —a young's laughter and a mother's call.

"Eek." Kailani scrambles up.

I laugh and urge her back into the water, following right behind her.

~

Kailani

. . .

WE DIVE UNDER THE WATERFALLS. Khrys swims for our clothing while I hang back and watch the family on the bank of the crystalline pool. They are a blended family—three Zandian males and one human female with twin boys— mixed species, maybe three solar cycles old—splashing in the shallow waters. The sight is completely foreign to me.

The human, indeed, appears free. She sits on a blanket spread on the ground, eating food from silver containers with two of the Zandians while the third stands at the water's edge supervising the children. Her repose is casual. There's a smile on her face. And I can't tell what she's eating, but it looks like real, whole food—not the gel packs I've been eating in space or the protein bars I was fed on Kraa.

My stomach suddenly rumbles.

Khrys climbs out of the water, beautifully unabashed at his nudity, and waves to the family. They wave back. I watch his muscles ripple as he steps into his clothing then picks up mine and walks around the bank in my direction. I swim over and climb out, shaking off the water droplets and letting his large body shield me from view as I dress.

"Who are they?" I ask, peeking around him, fascinated by what I see. They appear happy. I've never seen happy beings before. Especially not a human.

"A Zandian family. Come, I'll introduce you."

"You know them?"

"Zandia is small. I don't know them well, but I recognize them." Khrys hands me my shoes, and I slip them on. He takes my hand in his, and we walk over to the blanket.

The three stand to greet us. In the pool, the other Zandian scoops up the children and carries them over.

"Greetings." Khrys lifts his arm with his elbow bent at ninety degrees. The Zandians reflect the same gesture. "This is Kailani. She arrived on Zandia this planet rotation."

139

"I'm Riya." The female shocks me by speaking for the group. "And these are my mates, Jax

Tarren, and Ronan."

I try to keep my eyes from bulging in my head. "All three are your mates?"

Her smile is almost sultry. "Human females are lucky on Zandia." She trails her fingers over the rigid abs of Tarren, the shirtless Zandian who was down at the water with the young. He's tall, and his face is badly scarred. I would find him frightening if it weren't for the familiar and almost possessive way she touches him. "We can have more than one. They're desperate to repopulate and spread their genes around."

She touches the heads of the children. Both boys have lighter skin—somewhere between the light purple of the Zandians and her human coloring, tiny horns on top of their heads.

"This is Tarrian and Rylan, our boys."

"I want to go back to the water," one of the boys begs, tugging on his father's arm.

"I'll take you," Jax offers. "Race you to the edge." All three take off running, Jax jogging easily along as the little boys pump their legs vigorously.

I watch, fascinated.

"Are you hungry? My mates packed enough food for all of Zandia."

"Well, the boys require food at an alarming rate," Ronan explains. "Alarming for us, anyway. Just when we got used to how much an adult human needs to eat, we had to learn never to let a halfling's blood sugar dip."

"Do they eat a lot?" Khrys sounds surprised. He considers me with a warm gaze, and I find myself blushing, guessing at his thoughts.

"I would love to eat," I admit.

"Sit down," she urges, and we all sink to the blanket. She opens all the little metal boxes and places them in front of me. "These are heirloom tomatoes, originally from Earth. King Zander's mate Lamira was originally an ag farm slave, and she's shown Zandians how to farm since the human population requires food."

I pop one of the small red fruits in my mouth, and it explodes with juices and flavor. "Mmm," I moan. "Sweet Mother Earth, I've never tasted anything so good in my life."

Khrys picks up some kind of berry and lifts it to my lips, wanting to feed me. "Have you tried lemonberries? They're not from Earth, but they are delicious." I hold his gaze as I take it, savoring the moment, which is shimmering and unreal to me.

I take some kind of fluffy bread and bite into it, groaning at the delicious taste and texture. For a few moments, I just eat, absorbing the wondrous scene I am a part of—the incredible tastes, the casual, friendly conversation, the children's laughter and splashing in the water.

"Your young are healthy?" Khrys asks Tarren.

The enormous male shakes his head. "They both have been diagnosed, but we aren't seeing any effects yet. We made the decision to go on as if things are normal until they're not."

My gaze flies to Riya's face, and I catch a haunted quality I'd missed before. "They have the…" I— try to swallow— "the Z4-A virus? The one affecting your young?"

I look at Khrys, and he nods.

Unexpectedly, I burst into tears.

"Kailani." Khrys sounds alarmed. He tugs me into his lap.

I shake my head. "I'm all right." I don't know why I'm crying. Not because I'm sad for the children because I've already made up my mind. If I have the means to save those sweet beings, I'd do it in a heartbeat. It's more a release—all the fear and trauma of my past. The beauty before me. The kindness and openness of this marvelous blended family.

"You don't have to do it. You don't have to do anything," Khrys murmurs, misunderstanding my tears.

"Do what?" Riya asks.

"You don't have to," Khrys soothes. "I won't let it happen."

"What is it? What's wrong?" Riya asks.

"No, it's all right." I give a watery laugh. "I can do it. I'll do it right now." I push to stand from his lap. I felt like a victim before—like it was something being done to me. Now I see that it's clearly my choice. And knowing that makes all the difference. I'm no coward, and I've endured the worst kinds of pain. I know I can handle a little more. "I'm going to do it. Let's go back."

Khrys scrambles to his feet. "Are you sure?"

I nod. "I'm sure."

CHAPTER 13

ailani

"I WANT TO DONATE. I'll give you my blood and cells."

I squeeze Khrys' hand tightly, but my voice doesn't shake. "Khrys convinced me to do it, and it's because of him that I… offer myself to you."

This time my voice cracks. But I hold my chin high as I look at the array of Zandians before me, warriors and important beings. The king.

"I beg, in return, you forgive him for what he did. I'll give you blood whenever you want it." I hope I'm not overdoing it, but I'm desperate to convince them to let Khrys go free— and be with me.

Then I bow, like I saw Khrys do at the waterfall with the family there, showing proper deference to the king. Beside me, Khrys offers the Zandian gesture with his arm and bends down as well.

As we wait to hear our fate, I glance at my Zandian

143

warrior. His handsome face, so full of worry but also full of love, makes me melt.

"I love you no matter what," I whisper. "You're my mate."

"Did she call you her mate, Captain Khrys?" The king, whose ears are clearly as good as mine, steps closer. His voice isn't cruel, but I don't want him to be angry with me. He sounds like a being who has power and is used to wielding it as necessary.

Khrys stands. "Yes," he says. "I have not pierced her yet, but I claimed her on the ship. I intend to request permission to take her as my official mate and care for her for the rest of our lives." He puts his arm around me. "And if you give me the chance, I will serve Zandia with all of my heart, to the best of my ability."

I notice that Khrys' voice has lost a certain weight and tension that it held, even in our good moments together. He sounds confident and bold, instead of slightly on edge and sad.

I think the king notices, too, because he tilts his head and examines Khrys carefully.

"And I'll definitely keep giving you the best possible blood and you know, bone marrow or whatever you need, if you do," I add quickly, snaking an arm around him. "Because my adrenaline and cortisol levels will be within the desired ranges, I'm sure of it, if I'm allowed to be with Khrys." My whole body trembles with anxiety, and truth be told, I need to feel Khrys next to me in order not to pass out or fall into anxiety. I grab him and try not to hyper-ventilate.

"See?" I manage to hold up my wrist. The stupid armband shows all green lights. I don't know what they mean, but apparently, they indicate my health status.

Dr. Daneth makes a sound of approval. "That's very good. Much faster than I expected, given her initial condition."

The king looks at us both, eyes traveling over our faces. "Hmm." He nods to himself. "Dr. Daneth, please take her to the med bay."

I don't know if this means yes, he accepted my deal, or whether it means *veck you*, we do what we want, and we'll still throw Khrys in prison.

But I've offered myself up, and I won't take it back.

The stiff Zandian from the med bay comes toward me. "I am pleased that you changed your mind," he says without intonation, but the briskness of his movements indicate that he is indeed excited. "Please come with me." He points ahead. "One of our young is near death, and we need your antibodies as quickly as possible."

I pause and look back. "Please. I-I need Khrys. Can he be with me for it?" Now my voice trembles. I want to be brave, but there's no telling what will happen with me when I see the needles. Khrys makes me feel strong, though. He makes it all bearable.

There's a long terrible silence, and then the king says, "Yes. Go with your mate, Captain Khrys."

I exhale in relief and reach to take Khrys' outstretched hand. "Oh, thank you, thank you," I cry out, but I've buried my face in Khry's shoulder, and I don't know if the king can hear me. All I know is that finally, my life is starting to come together in a way I'd never dreamed possible.

"Captain Khrys, return next planet rotation," the King orders. "There are still some issues I must discuss with you."

"Yes, my lord," agrees Khrys. His voice is as full of relief as mine, though. It's clear that even if the king is still angry, Khrys' fate won't be a bad one. And we'll be together, which is the most important thing in the universe.

KHRYS

Kailani looks terrified, but she sits on the smooth bench and lays her arm out flat on the shining table as instructed by Doctor Daneth. I'm beside her, holding her other hand.

Bayla turns to us, her smile gentle. "I know you're scared." She touches Kailaini's shoulder. Her voice is low and reassuring. "First we'll give you a numbing agent, so you don't feel pain. Then we'll use a series of needles to extract blood and bone marrow. You'll feel pressure, but it won't hurt. Afterward your arm will be sore for a few solar cycles, but it will heal up like nothing happened."

"Okay. I can do this." Kailani's has a death grip on my fingers. "I want to help."

"It is an enormous help. You could be the answer." Bayla pulls a small holo device from her pocket. "Let me show you something, Kailani."

She taps, and an image flickers to life. I lean over, too, and she hands me the device, so I can view it clearly and hold it up for Kailani to see.

"This is a Zandian young before the sickness."

On the screen, an impossibly small halfling being runs up to a human woman, his arms full of branches.

"Mama!" He cries out, his small face bright with excitement. "Look at what I found! I'm going to build a huge fort."

He drops his bounty, and the woman scoops him up into her arms. He giggles and wiggles and wraps his small purple arms around her neck.

Then a new image plays. It's the same boy, but now he's listless and ill, breathing roughly, eyes closed. His mother's face is pinched and tear-stained. "He's getting worse," she

146

whispers to the viewer. "His breathing is harder. I just don't know…"

The holo zooms in on the boy's face. It's pale and the skin is damp. He's a million light years away from the robust child running and playing.

Bayla takes the holo device back. "That's just one example. Dozens of our young have fallen ill. They may die. They're the future of Zandia. And of humans." She touches Kailani's hand. "We believe your blood has antibodies that can save them, Kailani."

"Do it now. I'm not scared anymore." Kailani takes a deep breath. "I want to help."

The doctor comes back. "You're not going to flinch or pull away, are you?" He has his perpetual serious look on his face. "It's important for you to stay still during the procedure, and I know you don't like to be tied down."

Understatement. I wait for Kailani to freak out, but she doesn't.

"No." Kailani shakes her head. "I'll stay right here. I won't move."

I squeeze her hand reassuringly, and she smiles at me.

She barely twitches when the doctor rubs anesthetic on her arm. And she looks right at the needle when it breeches her skin.

I'm mesmerized to watch her bright red blood flow up into the tube, and I anxiously check her face—but she's all right. She looks pleased.

"You can take more," she offers.

"That's all we need." The doctor finishes the draw and moves away to a table. He puts a vial into a machine that whirs and beeps.

"Everything is within parameters and normal. Thank you, Kailani. This is exactly what we needed!" He's uncharacteristically excited. "This is perfect." Dr. Daneth looks at Bayla. "Can you ready the second extractor?"

"This second needle is larger," Bayla warns us. "Maybe you want to shut your eyes? It won't hurt, but it might upset you to watch?"

"I *want* to watch." Kailani's voice is firm. "I *want* to see the magic stuff that comes from me that is going to help the babies." A tear forms at the corner of her eye. "I'm made of good things, Khrys." She starts to cry. "For so long, I was just a tool. Now I'm more than that. I want to see all the good things. So I know they're real."

I wipe her tears with my fingers. "Sweet little warrior, you're full of amazing things." I kiss her gently. "And I'll show you every day how amazing you are."

Somehow my voice is a little shaky, too. *Veck*, maybe I've been infected by her emotions. My eyes are a little hazy.

"All right, last needle, now." The doctor approaches.

Kailani takes a deep breath and doesn't move a muscle during the process.

When it's over, I gather her into my arms. "You did that. You are incredible."

"It didn't even hurt," she whispers into my ear. "And I'm here. And nothing bad happened to me."

"Nothing bad will ever happen to you," I promise her. "I'll make sure of it."

"You can take her home," the doctor interrupts. "Ensure she gets plenty of nutrients, including these vitamin tubes." He hands over a packet. "Now, if you'll excuse me, I'm going to take these immediately to my lab and get to work." He begins to arrange a kit and bustles around the lab.

"Kailani, you'll need to come back in three planet rotations for a follow up," Bayla says, putting a small bandage on the puncture sites. "Just so we can make sure everything is all right."

"Okay." Kailani smiles.

I know she can walk just fine, but I scoop her up into my arms anyway. "I'm taking you to my domicile," I tell her. "Our domicile, now. We can get a nicer one now that you're here with me."

"I don't care what it looks like." She wraps her arms around my neck. "As long as we're together."

The sun is warm on my neck as I stride across the square. Beings are watching us, but I don't care, and I definitely don't stop for introductions. They'll get to meet Kailani soon enough, and right now, I have just one thing on my mind.

"You spoke of good things inside you," I murmur into her ear. "I have a *really* good thing I plan to put inside you just as soon as we're alone."

"Oooh, I like that good thing," she says immediately, biting my ear. "I want you to fill me with it at least three or four times this planet rotation."

I growl, and my cock hardens in my breeches. "This and every planet rotation, little warrior. And I'll probably need to spank you a few times, too, to remind you to behave properly now that you're a Zandian citizen."

"Of course," she agrees. "I may need more than one lesson."

I can oblige.

CHAPTER 14

 ailani

His domicile isn't rich or fancy, but the set of two rooms—a main living space with a sleep couch and a separate washroom are clean and organized. I look around, curious, running my finger over a smooth bench, checking the view from the window, which overlooks a busy Zandian thoroughfare below.

"I like it." I turn to him and smile. "It has everything we need."

"I suppose it's a little better than the cave on Dentron." He comes up to me and runs a finger down my cheek.

"Oh, there were a few things about the cave that I liked." I push my body into his, so my breasts contact his tunic.

"The rocks?" He tears off his tunic, and his glorious muscled body comes into view.

I shrug.

"Perhaps the dried branches. I hear humans like those."

He discards his breeches, and although I've seen his cock on numerous occasions, the sight of it makes me dizzy with need. "Strip for me, little warrior."

I pull down my gauzy garment. "It wasn't the branches. Try again."

"The view."

"Oh, I like this view, believe me." I smile at his amazing naked body. "I'd gladly see it all the time." I dart away when he reaches out for me. "I'll look at it from here, so I can see the whole thing."

He laughs. "Enough teasing. Get that delectable little body on the bed, all fours, and present your ass to your master."

"That's supposed to be you?" I raise a brow.

Then I scream in laughter as he moves like lightning and snatches me up.

"You know it is, little one." He sits down and pulls me over his lap. "Unfortunately for you, I'll have to remind you about it with the palm of my hand."

He slaps my ass hard, once and again. "Humans on Zandia need to be obedient to their guardians. You've got just enough sass that I'll have to spank you often to keep you docile."

"Ow!" I yelp although I like the sting, which reminds me that incredible orgasms are on the way.

"Twenty of these," he decides, "will probably be enough to convince you to present your pretty little ass to me immediately when I ask."

He spanks me over and over. "Next time I ask, I expect you to obey me instantly."

"Yes, Master," I gasp, as the burn starts to grow stronger. "I promise. Please!"

He rubs my bottom. "Are you ready to do as I asked?"

"Yes, please," I whimper, and once he lets me go, I hurry to scramble over and get on all fours, spreading my legs wide enough, so he can see my pussy—just the way he likes it.

"Very good," he murmurs, coming up and rubbing my tingling buttocks. "Tilt your hips up just a bit. Yes, like that. Remember that pose for next time."

"Yes, Master," I whisper, adjusting my body. "I want you."

"And you'll have me. In just a little bit."

He gets up from the bed, and I hear some clatter as he opens a cupboard.

"What are you doing?" I try to look over.

"Stay in position," he orders, his voice kind but firm, so I look back at the cover and ensure that my hips are nice and high.

When he comes back over, he touches my back softly. "Dr. Daneth recommended this as a tool to use on human females. I'll see how you react to it." He drops something onto the bed near my calf, but I can't see what it is.

I make a small noise of uncertainty, and he chuckles. "I think you'll end up liking it. It's a plug that goes…" he taps one finger on my exposed anus, "here."

I squeak and try to close my legs, but he's anticipated this, and grasps my thighs with his powerful hands.

"Relax," he soothes me. "Have I done anything that you don't end up enjoying?"

"No, Master," I whisper.

"Then trust me."

"Yes, Master." I'm nervous about this plug, but he's not wrong: Everything intimate he does ends up bringing me immense pleasure, so I decide to relax and enjoy this new experience with him.

"I've lubricated it." He presses something cool at my

entrance. "Keep your muscles loose, and it will go in more easily, Kailani."

"Eeek!" I twist my hips instinctively.

He spanks my ass. "Stay still." Then I hear the click of a lid, and he drizzles some liquid onto my bottom. "I'll get you used to it first with my fingers."

He uses his index finger to rub the lotion on my buttocks, and eventually works his finger to my anus. When he presses it inside, I make a little moan but attempt to relax my body as instructed. At first, it feels tight and foreign, but as he works his finger in and out, over and over, first deeper, then teasing the rim of my anus, it starts to feel… good.

Really good.

I squirm and gasp. "Khrys."

"You like that?" He chuckles. "That's what I expected."

He pushes a second finger in with the first.

"Ow, oh." I suck in my breath—it hurts for one second, then it feels even better than before.

He works his fingers in and out with one hand and uses the other one to reach under and play with my nipples. It isn't long before I'm moving my hips up rhythmically, wanting more from him.

"Hmmm. I think you're ready." He pulls his fingers out. "Ask me for the plug, Kailani. You won't get my cock today until you've enjoyed a good session with the plug, so I suggest you ask me very nicely and convince me to put it into your pretty little ass."

"Please Khrys." I gulp. "I want that…" my face gets hot. I don't want to ask for it.

He slaps my ass. "What do you want?"

"I want—please put the plug into my ass." My voice is small, but I get the words out.

"Of course." He puts the plug at the entrance of my ass.

"I'd be delighted to plug you, little human." This time, because my body is prepared, the plug goes right in.

"It will hurt for a bit, then it will feel good again," he warns me.

"Ouch!" The rim of my anus burns as the thicker part of the plug breeches my body. I'm about to ask him to remove it, when the rest of it slides in, leaving me feeling full.

The pain fades. Khrys grasps the plug and begins to work it gently in my body—pulling it part way out, pushing it in. Twisting it.

Each sensation sets my nerve endings on fire in a way I've never known, and I know I need to come soon.

"Kyrs, please," I gasp.

He pushes the plug all the way back in and spanks me once right on top of it. I almost explode right there.

"Oh, stars," I mutter.

"*Veck*, Kailani, I can't wait any longer." He gets behind me, and his cock pushes at my pussy. "Are you ready for a good *vecking*?"

"Stars, please, yes."

Like always, his huge cock seems like it will barely fit, even when I'm wet, and then when he's inside me, I never want it to end.

He grabs my hips and pumps me, softly and then harder.

"Does it feel even better with that plug in your ass?" He pulls his cock out and drives it back into me, so hard I brace with both elbows and forearms on the bed.

"Yes," I whisper. The scent of my arousal and his fill the air—an intoxicating scent that only turns me on more. "Yes."

Then there's no need for words as the rhythm takes over. We move together as one until the pleasure explodes over me, and I cry out my joy as he comes, too.

The feeling of his release spurs me on to even greater

heights of pleasure, and I come again and again, my whole body suffused with miraculous sensations.

After a moment, he rolls over and flops down beside me, panting. I'm bathed in sweat and delirious with happiness, and I have just enough energy to fall onto my side and push into him. One hand on his thigh, one cupping his buttock, I lie there just existing and enjoying this moment with him.

Khrys.

My mate.

Time floats by, and the sun beams come through the window, lighting on our bodies, making everything glow, at least when I bother to open my eyes for a second here and there just to look at him.

But then—

Eeeeek.

A strange sound comes from a cabinet across the room.

Eeeeerp.

"Khrys?" I rouse myself from my delirious haze. "Is there something—what's that sound?" I prop up onto one elbow. "It's coming from over there."

"Huh?" He blinks.

I smile—he's as drunk on this feeling as I am.

"There's a sound. I just don't know—is everything okay?"

Sqeeeeee.

Suddenly, my eyes widen. "Oh, my stars, Khrys—is it…"

I don't even want to hope, but it sure sounds a lot like my Whimmie.

He clears his throat and manages to drag himself to his feet. "I was going to wait until we'd relaxed a little bit, but I did something. For you."

He pulls on his breeches and fetches a small container with air holes from behind the bench. "I got permission from our ag director to keep her for you. They checked her for disease, and she doesn't have any, and she can't reproduce so…"

He opens the crate, and there's a blur of purple and blue.

Squeeeek! The creature races across the room and leaps onto the bed. In a second, it's in my arms, licking my face with that strange rough tongue. It makes a rumbling sound from deep within its body.

"My Whimmie!" My heart leaps, and I laugh, holding her close. "Oh, Khrys. You got her for me. She's here." I hug her and kiss the top of her head. "And she's all clean, too. Look how pretty she is!"

Khrys rolls his eyes. "She's tolerable." He crosses his arms. "For the record, I still consider them vermin. But this one can live...here." He wrinkles his nose. "With us. For as long...as you want it."

He's clearly not thrilled. Whimmie looks at him and growls. Then she jumps to the windowsill and arranges herself into a little bundle to watch the activities.

Khrys crosses the room and sits beside me. "She only bit me once when I fetched her from the ag center," he says, holding up his hand. "I bet she'll start to like me eventually."

"Oh, I'm sure." I take his hand. "Where did she bite you? Want me to kiss it?"

"Never mind the hand. You can kiss me here." Khrys gestures to his breeches. "On a very certain area. I know that will make me feel better."

"One way to find out." I wink at him.

And the rest of the planet rotation goes very, very well.

EPILOGUE

 *hrys*

"It's so beautiful," Kailani breathes as we file into the royal garden and take our places. It's true, the garden is exquisite, filled with flowers and fruit trees, vines and berries all around the perimeter. Hundreds of Zandians gather within the rebuilt palace walls for the ceremony and celebration.

Back when we lived on the Palatial Pod before we recovered our planet from the Finn, King Zander—who still went by Prince Zander—held a banquet for any and all living Zandians on one planet rotation every lunar cycle. We all had the pleasure of dining with the prince and his royal team. He sat on his throne and heard complaints and made rulings.

Now that we're back on Zandia and the population has grown and spread, formal gatherings happen here and are often by invite only.

Today, Kailani and I are special guests.

King Zander stands at the podium and flips a switch to

project his voice. "Greetings Zandians. And you all know by now, when I say Zandians, I include those born into our species as well as those adopted, mated and naturalized. He lets that settle in, his gaze sweeping across the mixed crowd of Zandians and humans and halflings.

"We are here today to celebrate the total and complete eradication of the Z4-A virus from our planet. Every being infected with the virus has now made a full recovery. There are no new cases of infection, and we have a vaccine to ensure we will never have another outbreak. Please join me in honoring those who dedicated themselves to finding a cure and caring for the ill. May I first present to you my first honoree, the royal physician, Dr. Daneth."

The crowd applauds as Dr. Daneth walks onto the dais and bows.

"His mate and assistant, Bayla."

Bayla comes to the dais, curtsies and takes her place beside Dr. Daneth.

"Captain Khrys, the warrior whose methods may have been questionable but who sought and found the answers to a cure off-planet."

I step up and bow, never taking my gaze from my beautiful mate.

"His mate, Kailani, who repeatedly offered her blood and cells up for our experimentation until Dr. Daneth and his team were able to develop the cure."

Kailani climbs the stairs to the dais and drops into a graceful curtsy then comes to stand beside me. I wrap my arm around her waist and tuck her against my side, protectively, even though she requires no protection.

King Zander goes on to recognize other members of the team, but I stop listening because Kailani tips her face up to mine. "Dr. Daneth discovered something new in the last blood sample I gave," she whispers.

On my other side, Bayla cranes her neck to see Kailani around my chest.

I frown. "What is it?" I murmur back, my heart starting to pound.

"I'm pregnant." Her smile could light a thousand moons.

"Stars," I murmur, touching her face. "Is it true?" I turn to look to Bayla, who is also smiling.

Kailani nods.

King Zander finishes delivering accolades, and the crowd cheers. I pick up my little warrior to carry her off the dais, suddenly not trusting her feet to touch the ground.

"What are you telling me?" I spin her around.

She giggles, the most beautiful glow lighting her face.

"We're having a young? Truly?"

Stars, I never wanted young, but now, the thought fills me with so much pride and joy, I can hardly contain it.

"Should you be home in bed? What do we need to do?" I'm suddenly alarmed by the need to protect her at all costs.

Bayla is still near us, and she laughs. "She's fine. She can keep working with you as an assistant trainer until the baby comes. But after that, you'll have to find a new assistant."

I stare into my mate's beautiful blue eyes, the garden spinning around me. "You've made me so happy, little warrior."

She tucks her head onto my shoulder and kisses my neck. "I'm happy, too."

"Before I met you, my life was falling apart. My honor was in tatters, I hated myself for my mistakes. I couldn't imagine a future that had any possibilities of joy. This planet rotation, I was honored by my king, alongside my incredible mate who helped me put my ghosts in the past. The one who is the biggest hero on our planet. And now she tells me we're going to have a young, to become a family?" My eyes burn.

"I was thinking...if we have a boy—let's name him Kyl after your brother."

The familiar pain from thinking of Kyl lances through my heart, but it's followed by such a flood of warmth that the pain dissipates, spreading and eventually easing until all I feel is love. With Kailani by my side, I've been able to let go of the trauma that plagued me from his death. I've been able to return to my position as a trainer without the hiccups in confidence I used to have.

"Yes," I manage to say. "Yes. I would love that."

"I love you," she murmurs against my skin.

"I love you so much, little warrior. Thank you. For all you've done for me. And for all you've done for Zandia."

"Khrys," she murmurs huskily.

"Yes, little warrior?"

"Take me home. I'd like to feel your appreciation... physically."

My horns stiffen, and I nearly trip in my haste to maneuver through the crowd to the garden gates.

"I'll show you my appreciation all night long, little warrior."

"Mmm," she murmurs, flicking her tongue against my earlobe and making my horns throb. "I was counting on it."

End

Thank you for reading *Stolen by the Zandian*!

If you enjoyed the book, we would really appreciate a review. Your reviews are invaluable to indie authors in marketing books so we can keep book prices down.

READ ALL THE ZANDIAN BRIDES
SERIES

Night of the Zandians
    Bought by the Zandians
    Mastered by the Zandians
    Zandian Lights
    Kept by the Zandian
    Claimed by the Zandian
    Stolen by the Zandian

WANT FREE RENEE ROSE BOOKS?

Go to http://subscribepage.com/alphastemp to sign up for Renee Rose's newsletter and receive a free copy of *Theirs to Protect, Owned by the Marine*, *Theirs to Punish, The Alpha's Punishment, Disobedience at the Dressmaker's* and *Her Billionaire Boss*. In addition to the free stories, you will also get special pricing, exclusive previews and news of new releases.

ABOUT REBEL WEST

Alexis Alvarez writes hot kink with doms so sexy you'll swoon! She's into photography and travel, and when she's not figuring out ways to get her main characters together, she's out with her camera looking for inspiration. Find her under her other pen name, Rebel West, where she writes kinky alien romances and the Zandian Bride Series with her writing partner Renee Rose.

Read More by Rebel West / Alexis Alvarez

Zandian Brides Series (with co-writer Renee Rose)
 Night of the Zandians
 Bought by the Zandians
 Mastered by the Zandians
 Zandian Lights
 Kept by the Zandian
 Claimed by the Zandian
 Stolen by the Zandian

Vampire Romance:
 Her Vampire Temptation (part of the Midnight Doms Series)
 All Soul's Night (A Midnight Doms Vampire Anthology)

Sci-Fi Romance

Conquered by the Alien Prince: Luminar Masters, Book 1

Contemporary Romance
   Perfect Match
   A Handful of Fire
   Boston
   Dream Girl

Kinky/BDSM Romance
   Hammered (Enemies to Lovers Romance, part of the Hard N' Dirty Series)
   Heating Up The Holidays (Anthology of Kinky Stories)
   His Firm Direction
   Casey's Choice
   Capturing Kate
   Myka and the Millionaire
   Return

Find Alexis Alvarez (aka Rebel West) on Social Media

Alexis Alvarez Amazon Author Page: https://www.amazon.com/Alexis-Alvarez/e/B0107LJQEM
   Rebel West Author Page: https://www.amazon.com/Rebel-West/e/B07B866MY9
   Newsletter: https://goo.gl/forms/iVRhZbk2s0mz8v6h2

OTHER TITLES BY RENEE ROSE

Sci-Fi

Zandian Masters Series

His Human Slave

His Human Prisoner

Training His Human

His Human Rebel

His Human Vessel

His Mate and Master

Zandian Pet

Their Zandian Mate

His Human Possession

Zandian Brides

Night of the Zandians

Bought by the Zandians

Mastered by the Zandians

Zandian Lights

Kept by the Zandian

Claimed by the Zandian

Stolen by the Zandian

Other Sci-Fi

The Hand of Vengeance

Her Alien Masters

Chicago Bratva

The Director

The Fixer

Vegas Underground Mafia Romance

King of Diamonds

Mafia Daddy

Jack of Spades

Ace of Hearts

Joker's Wild

His Queen of Clubs

Dead Man's Hand

Wild Card

More Mafia Romance

Her Russian Master

The Don's Daughter

Mob Mistress

The Bossman

Contemporary

Daddy Rules Series

Fire Daddy

Hollywood Daddy

Stepbrother Daddy

Master Me Series

Her Royal Master

Her Russian Master

Her Marine Master

Yes, Doctor

Double Doms Series

Theirs to Punish

Theirs to Protect

Holiday Feel-Good

Scoring with Santa

Saved

Other Contemporary

Black Light: Valentine Roulette

Black Light: Roulette Redux

Black Light: Celebrity Roulette

Black Light: Roulette War

Punishing Portia (written as Darling Adams)

The Professor's Girl

Safe in his Arms

Paranormal

Wolf Ranch Series

Rough

Wild

Feral

Savage

Fierce

Ruthless

Wolf Ridge High Series

Alpha Bully

Alpha Knight

Bad Boy Alphas Series

Alpha's Temptation

Alpha's Danger

Alpha's Prize

Alpha's Challenge

Alpha's Obsession

Alpha's Desire

Alpha's War

Alpha's Mission

Alpha's Bane

Alpha's Secret

Alpha's Prey

Alpha's Sun

Midnight Doms

Alpha's Blood

His Captive Mortal

Alpha Doms Series

The Alpha's Hunger

The Alpha's Promise

The Alpha's Punishment

Other Paranormal

The Winter Storm: An Ever After Chronicle

Regency

The Darlington Incident

Humbled

The Reddington Scandal

The Westerfield Affair

Pleasing the Colonel

Western

His Little Lapis

The Devil of Whiskey Row

The Outlaw's Bride

Medieval

Mercenary

Medieval Discipline

Lords and Ladies

The Knight's Prisoner

Betrothed

Held for Ransom

The Knight's Seduction

The Conquered Brides (5 book box set)

Renaissance

Renaissance Discipline

Manufactured by Amazon.ca
Bolton, ON